I0663773

# Her Country Heart Christmas Edition

## Sierra Creek Series Book 1

# Reggi Allder

# PRAISE
## Sierra Creek Series

**5 STARS AMAZON** "Great characters! I'm HOOKED!!! A seriously great book!! I am so happy it is a series."

**GOODREADS** "The interaction between the characters held my attention and I couldn't wait to find out what happened next. I don't want to spoil the ending for you by telling now, but it's so emotional it is well worth reading all the way through."

**5 STARS** "I loved it and didn't want the book to end!"

Copyright © Second Edition10-2024 Reggi Allder
All rights reserved. Except for use in a review, this book may not be reproduced or utilized in whole or in part in any form by any electronic, mechanical, or other means, known today or invented hereafter, xerography, photocopying, or any information storage or retrieval system and is forbidden without written permission.

This is a work of fiction. Names, characters, places, and incidents are the product of the author's imagination or are used fictitiously. Any resemblance to actual persons, living or dead, business establishments, or events is entirely coincidental. Cressmead Publishing.

ISBN 978-0-9921148-8-6

# DEDICATION

To Lee Lee, for his unfailing love, and to Gran, who always had time to listen whenever I needed her.

## ACKNOWLEDGMENTS

Thank you to all who work to bring food to our table.

Thank you to my great critique partners.

## Books by Reggi Allder

**Dangerous Series:**
Dangerous Web
Dangerous Denial
Dangerous Moves
Dangerous Money
Dangerous Moves
**Coming Next:** Dangerous Sisters
**Sierra Creek Series:**
Her Country Heart
His Country Heart
Our Country Heart
My Country Heart

**Other Books:**
**Shattered Rules**
**With Glowing Hearts**

# CHAPTER 1

**"Sierra** Creek," the driver shouted as the Greyhound bus came to an abrupt stop on the two-lane highway.

Amy Long pushed her hair behind her ears and grabbed her worn suitcase. Surprised to see her hand tremble, she seized the case with both hands and rushed toward the front of the bus.

A gust of hot wind slapped her face as she stepped outside. Gravel pelted her bare legs when the bus drove away. She squinted and read a faded road sign, *Sierra Creek population five thousand.* There wasn't a building in sight.

After years of living in the city, she'd forgotten how sweltering and desolate it was here. She'd vowed never to return home. Odd it was the first place that came to mind when she and her young son needed a fresh start.

With Granny gone, there was no family left to welcome her. She swallowed a sob. Maybe it was a mistake to come back.

The relentless afternoon sun beat down on her shoulders and her arms began to burn. San Francisco, the air-conditioned city, seemed a million miles away.

Impatient, she cleared her dry throat, wiped perspiration from her forehead, and groaned as the minutes ticked by. What wouldn't she give for some shade and a bottle of iced water?

With a sigh, she pulled out her smartphone and checked the time. Thirty minutes since she'd arrived at the bus stop and not a single car had gone by. Where was the arranged ride into town?

Granny's handyman was supposed to meet her. He apparently wasn't a stickler about being on time. She reminded herself she was in the California foothills, not in a busy metropolis where time was money.

The sound of a truck rumbled in the distance. With the back of her hand, she pushed her bangs out of her eyes and squinted. Hopeful, she watched the pick-up come closer. A shiny black Ford F150 with an extended cab pulled up in front of her.

"Amy," a man yelled through the open window as his brown hair fell casually over a high forehead and deep-set blue eyes sparkled in the sunlight. She moved nearer and stared at his wide cheekbones, square jaw, and full lips. *About thirty?*

A flutter of recognition stirred in her as palpable charm radiated from his broad smile, Wyatt Cameron.

His muscular arms flexed as his huge hands squeezed the steering wheel. "Don't just stand there. Get in."

Surprised by his gruffness, she stepped back.

"I heard you need a ride into town," he said quietly as if he understood her reaction. "I'm Wyatt."

"Hi, good to see you again." Even now, her cheeks burned with the memory of him. As she stared her heartbeat increased and her breathing quickened. "Granny's handyman is going to give me a ride."

"You could say that's me. Toss your suitcase in the back and get in the truck."

She shook the pebbles from her flip-flops and picked up her suitcase. Filled with everything she and her son might need, she grunted and struggled to lift the enormous bag high enough to push it into the raised truck bed.

Wyatt hopped out of the cab and brushed by her. With a sharp intake of breath, she took in his fresh just-out–of–the-shower scent.

Effortlessly, he tossed the bag into the truck.

She quickly hauled herself into the vehicle and slammed the door. "Nice truck. Beautiful upholstery," she said trying for casual conversation. She ran her hand over the black and white leather seat.

"It's custom. Had it done in Sacramento by a guy who specializes in tuck and roll seats."

"Really nice."

*Pretty fancy truck for a handyman.* The job must pay better than she thought. For some reason, she believed Granny's handyman would be an old retired guy gnarled from too much sun and hard work, not the hunk sitting next to her.

"Where's your son? Thought he'd be with you."

"He's staying with a friend of mine in San Francisco. Bobby's only four. I thought it'd be better if I took care of a few things here before he comes to the farm." She paused. "It's only been a few hours since I left and I already miss him."

She sighed, leaned back, and let the air-conditioned breeze wash over her. The purr of the truck's engine was soothing and her breathing slowed.

"Thanks for picking me up. If you drop me at my grandmother's farm, I'll…"

"It's too late for that. We can't keep Judge Wilcox waiting."

"I need a shower and a change of clothes before I see him." She yanked on her cutoff jeans and pulled on her pink tank top. No matter how hard she tugged they were both too short. "I can't wear these clothes in front of a judge."

Wyatt quickly scanned her before returning his gaze to the road. "You should have thought of that when you dressed this morning."

"I thought there would be time to clean up and put on something more—more appropriate. How could I know the bus would be late? My ride was late too," she said pointedly.

He mumbled an expletive under his breath then said, "You'll just have to deal with it." His features hardened and his lips tightened.

The plea for him to change his mind stuck in her throat. The set of his jaw told her it wouldn't do any good to ask him to reconsider.

As the vehicle roared down the highway, she found a comb in her purse and yanked it through her tangled hair. She dug in her bag, looking for a ponytail holder. No luck. Still wishing she had time to shower and change, she applied pink lipstick, breathed the cool air, and resisted looking at Wyatt.

*** 

Sierra Creek, the gold rush town, looked much the same as the last time she was there, two years earlier. She smiled, comforted by the fact that there was something in her life that hadn't changed.

Main Street, had the turn of the twentieth-century buildings, gleaming with fresh paint. "Open" signs looked out from retail stores, trying to entice shoppers to come in and browse.

No big box stores allowed. The same shops she remembered as a kid were still there, including Sol's Barber Shop, Andy's General Store, and Sophie's Ice Cream Parlor, where Amy and her friends had spent many hours talking over ice cream sodas and diet cokes.

The huge columned courthouse at the end of the street looked like it could be part of a nineteen-fifties movie set. Was it a good idea to bring Bobby to a town that time forgot? Did she have a choice?

Wyatt dropped her off at the curb in front of the courthouse and went to park the truck. With shoulders squared, she forced her head high and walked up the steps. Suddenly nervous, she hesitated at the front door.

Without warning, her throat tightened. She gasped, unable to get her breath. Granny was gone. She'd never see her beloved grandmother again. The realization slammed into her like a fist to her chest. Rooted in place, she struggled against a surge of tears.

"Come on. We're late." Wyatt caught hold of her arm.

"No. I—" She held her hand to her mouth to stop a cry.

"Judge Wilcox is waiting."

Wyatt led her into the building and to a room off of the rotunda.

Everyone in the chamber stared when she entered, and the room went unexpectedly silent.

"Mrs. Long, I presume."

She nodded at the sound of the judge's deep voice. "Yes, Your Honor." Her voice cracked. She cleared her throat and yanked on the back of her shorts.

"Take a seat." The man's brown eyes narrowed as he scrutinized her.

"Yeah. I mean yes, sir." She sank into the nearest chair and didn't look at anyone in the room.

"Now that you are all here, we can start." The judge still glared at her. "This is the last will and testament of Mary Louise McCarthy."

Amy gasped.

"Do you need something, Mrs. Long?" the judge asked.

"No."

"Then I will continue. I, Mary McCarthy, hereby revoke all former wills and codicils."

Amy leaned back in the chair and closed her eyes against the truth of Granny's death.

The judge's voice droned on, but she had difficulty concentrating. Memories of her grandmother flooded her. Granny was always smiling, always cheerful, and always kind, even when, as a teenager, Amy had rebelled and wouldn't listen to reason.

Her grandmother was her rock, the problem solver, the woman with overgenerous patience. Together they'd managed to find an answer to Amy's many troubling situations. But today, there would be no resolution. If only she could speak to Granny one last time and tell her how much she loved her.

"I direct my executor, Wyatt Cameron, to pay my enforceable unsecured debts and funeral expenses, the cost of my last illness, and the operating expense of administering my estate. I direct him, without apportionment against any beneficiary or other person, to pay all estate, inheritance, and succession taxes (including any interest and penalties thereon) payable by reason of my death," the judge continued.

She heard disjointed words that floated in the air as she bit her lower lip and pressed her hand tightly against her mouth. Did the judge just say Wyatt Cameron was the executor of Granny's will? She shook her head. *I must have heard that wrong.*

"I bequeath fifteen hundred dollars to the Sierra Creek Methodist Church and one thousand dollars to the Sacramento Society for the Prevention of Cruelty to Animals," the man continued. "To my good friend Sophie Danelavich, I leave my Windsor rocking chair and the grandfather clock she always admired."

There were other small bequests, but Amy couldn't concentrate enough to hear them. "Focus," she said and forced her eyes open to pay attention.

The judge glanced at her, and almost as if he understood she was having trouble following him, he spoke more slowly, "I thank Wyatt Cameron for his help. It allowed me to continue to live in my home. My bequest gives him the use of my cottage and barn for as long as he needs them. And I leave half ownership of my farm, including all buildings and land, to Wyatt Cameron."

"No," Amy whispered.

"That can't be right." Wyatt jumped up.

"It is correct, Mr. Cameron. Do not interrupt this court again or I will ask you to leave my chambers. Do you understand?"

"Yeah. Sorry Your Honor."

"Mr. Cameron, take your seat."

"I didn't know, Amy." Wyatt leaned closer and reached for her.

"Get away from me." She yanked her hand from his.

A murmur went through the room.

"Silence." Judge Wilcox slammed his gavel down on his desk. "Everyone, settle down."

The whispers and mumbling slowed.

Amy wiped tears from her eyes. Granny betrayed her and Bobby. Why would she give half the farm to Wyatt? He wasn't blood kin, not even a distant cousin. He was just—nobody.

Her grandmother wouldn't do that. He had tricked Granny into leaving half the property to him. He wouldn't get away with it, not if she could stop it.

"To Amy Long, I give all the rest of my tangible property, real and personal, and all the residue and remainder of my estate."

The judge cleared his throat and stood. "That concludes the reading. If any of you have questions, call my office and make an appointment to see me. Now everybody get."

He glanced from Amy to Wyatt. "Mrs. Long, I've set up a meeting for next Monday at two o'clock in my office for you and Mr. Cameron to complete the transfer of your grandmother's property."

Without waiting for her to agree to the appointed day and time, he left the chamber. It seemed that the meeting next Monday was not a request. It was a command.

People filed out of the room without speaking to her. She watched hoping to find a familiar face but didn't see one.

Wyatt's truck was parked at the curb in front of the building when she came out of the courthouse.

"I'll drive you to Granny's farm."

*Don't you mean your farm?* She bit back the caustic reply. A thief, the thought of sitting next to him in the truck turned her stomach. But with no cab or bus in town, a five-mile walk to Granny's house dragging a giant suitcase in one-hundred-degree heat wasn't appealing either. She squelched the need to tell him what he could do with his ride. With a hiss under her breath, she got in his truck and slammed the door shut.

"Did you say something?"

"No."

He looked unconvinced but started the engine without saying anything more.

A few minutes later, the Ford turned off the two-lane highway onto Star Route Three.

She waited for Granny's property to come into view at the end of the road. Had it been two years since she'd come home? It seemed like yesterday. How could everything look the same when her world had totally changed?

In anticipation, she sat forward. The apple orchards appeared first, the trees green-leafed and flushed with fruit almost ready to be harvested. No matter how many new brands of apples came on the market, the red delicious apple defined the fruit for her.

The white two-story traditional American farmhouse with its pointed gables and wraparound porch, so popular in the Sierra Foothills, glistened in the late afternoon. Her chest tightened at the sight.

Soon, the sun would be setting. So many times, she and Granny had sat on the porch peeling apples for applesauce as they watched the late afternoon sky turn orange.

Wyatt drove the truck into the driveway and turned off the engine. Anxious to get into the house, she reached into her pocket and felt for the key Granny had given her many years earlier.

"If you will get my suitcase out of the truck, I won't keep you. I'm sure you'd like to get home."

Wyatt's eyebrows rose as he turned to face her. "I thought you understood—I live here."

# CHAPTER 2

**"Your** grandmother's will gives me the right to stay on the farm as long as I want to," Wyatt said.

How stupid could Amy be? He owned half the farm. So, he could certainly live on it. She'd assumed he had a home somewhere else, anywhere but the farm. His taking half ownership of Granny's place was bad enough, but the thought of him living in her grandmother's home was unbearable.

The worn plank floor creaked when she walked into her childhood home. The familiar smell of lilac and pine still permeated the old place. She ran a shaking hand over the familiar pastel-flowered sofa and touched the blue and white granny square blanket her grandmother had knitted. It lay tossed on the corner of Grandpa's leather club chair just as it had when she'd first seen it as a scared six-year-old kid who'd come to live with her grandparents.

In a few days, Bobby would arrive on the farm. Slightly younger than she'd been when she came to live there, he also needed a haven from the problems in his young life just as she had when her mother had sent her to live on the farm.

Would Wyatt let her stay now that he was the executor and half-owner of the place? Could he turn her away even though she and Bobby had nowhere else to go? The question sent a jab of fear rushing through her.

She glanced around the room. Everything held a memory, a story of Granny, only deepening her sense of loss. Sorrow tightened her chest, threatening to stifle her breathing. She forced herself to inhale deeply.

Amy hadn't cried when she received the phone call that Granny was gone. She didn't want Bobby upset. Now, she swallowed a sob. She wouldn't let Wyatt see her cry now.

He had the right to stay in her home. No matter how angry that made her, she couldn't stop him. But she wouldn't let him see her tears.

***

Without the sun, the evening cooled. In the great room of the old house, Wyatt set a fire in the stone fireplace. She watched the muscles of his strong back flex as he lifted a huge oak log and placed it on the burning kindling. Her body reacted with a sudden shot of heat, but it was proximity to him, not the fire's warmth, that caused it.

"That should keep the cold out tonight." Wyatt brushed ash from his jeans and stretched his hands out to the fire, then turned and smiled.

Though anger pulsed in her, his magnetism called to her. Damn, her female response to his sex appeal. She moved toward him, stopped, moved back, and gave her head a quick shake. Granny must have felt the pull of his charisma too. Was that how he got her to sign over half of the farm to him?

"I make you uncomfortable."

"No. It's not that." She crossed her arm in a defensive motion and resisted moving further away from him. "I just thought I'd be alone," she said not wanting to admit the truth of his statement.

The corners of his mouth turned up slightly, not exactly a smile, but at least not a frown.

"I'm trying to remember what the judge said. I couldn't seem to focus when I was in his chamber," she whispered.

"The will said I'm the executor of your grandmother's estate and that I inherit half the property. I can live on the farm and use the barn for as long as I need it."

"But I—" Unable to think how she could contradict what he said, she stopped.

"Amy, I slept in the house when your grandmother was alive. And after she was gone there didn't seem to be a reason to move out." He hesitated. "Tomorrow, I'll make the old cottage in the backyard livable. Tonight, if you want to be alone, I can sleep in my truck."

The thought of him trying to rest, while tossing and turning, unable to fold his tall frame into a comfortable position in the truck's cab sent a genuine smile to her lips. But she said, "I wouldn't dream of it. You can sleep in the house. Uh—tonight."

With a nod, he walked toward the door.

"Are you leaving?"

"Your grandmother gave me something for you. It's in the truck."

The front door slammed shut when he left.

With a sigh, she sank onto the overstuffed sofa, leaned back, and closed her eyes. Pain throbbed in her temples.

As a handyman, Wyatt Cameron hadn't made much of a career for himself. Still, he'd helped

Granny stay in her home until the end. That would have counted for a lot if he hadn't ended up owning half of the farm.

Handsome, self-confident, she had to admit there was a rough charm about him. But what kind of man was he?

Granny trusted him. What did that mean? Had he enchanted the frail old woman and forced her into giving him half her land and control of the estate? Was her grandmother so trusting, so elderly that she didn't see a predator, a user? Had he been after control of the farm the whole time he helped her?

Images of Amy's ex-husband Robert flashed. He'd been able to smile charmingly while lying to her face. Both he and Wyatt were tall, handsome, outwardly charming specimens of men, but besides that, they were nothing alike. Or were they?

Gullible when she was young, she'd been easily duped by Robert's charm and good looks, unaware that those traits could mask selfishness and cruelty. She'd never again mistake charm for love or good looks for the sign of a good man.

The miserable relationship with her ex shouldn't color her view of Wyatt. Should it? Or could it make her wise enough to not let another charming liar fool her?

Feelings of guilt over her disastrous marriage hit her, she shook them away. After all, something wonderful had come out of it—Bobby.

She entered the kitchen with its worn hardwood floors, whitewashed walls, and white lace curtains. The plaque she'd given Granny for Christmas years earlier still hung on the wall next to the window.

"Grandma Cooks with Love," she read the sign out loud.

*Home.* Nothing said it like her grandmother's kitchen. Years earlier, in this room, she'd done chores, finished homework, and spun daydreams. With Granny, she'd spent hours cooking while talking and laughing. She wiped a wayward tear from her cheek.

Her stomach growled. Although she didn't feel hungry, she had to eat. The toast and coffee she'd had for breakfast weren't enough.

As she'd done a hundred times before, she opened the freezer, but this time she found it empty. Gone were the neatly labeled plastic boxes of soup, spaghetti, and lasagna meals that Granny always had there.

Amy found and opened a can of store-bought Minestrone soup, and put it in a pot to warm on the burner of the antique gas stove. A loaf of fresh sourdough bread sat on the kitchen table. Wyatt must have purchased that.

While the soup warmed, she set the table.

"There's food if you want it," she called to Wyatt. They ate in silence.

The hot liquid trickled down her throat as she scanned the kitchen. She could almost see her grandmother cooking at the stove; the aroma of homemade bread in the air, her smile filling the room. Amy stifled a cry and pushed her full bowl of soup away.

Wyatt emptied his bowl and took it to the kitchen sink, rinsed it and set it on the drain board.

"Here's a letter from your grandmother. She asked me to give it to you." He handed over a sealed pink envelope pulled from his jacket pocket.

"Thank you." Her hand trembled when she grabbed it.

"I'll leave you alone."

"Thanks."

Not ready to read the letter, she yanked her cell phone from the leather shoulder bag that hung on the back of the kitchen chair and put in Nan's number.

Worry sent a quiver through her. This would be Bobby's first night without her, the first time she'd been away from him since his birth. The wooden floor creaked as she paced and counted the rings waiting for someone to answer the cell.

"Hey," Nan said, sounding breathless.

"Hi, Nan."

"Amy, Bobby's fine. I know it's getting late, but we're playing ball in the backyard. Let me catch my breath." She paused. "Don't worry. He hasn't eaten anything that's not on the list you gave me."

"Thanks, Nan. I shouldn't worry." She sighed. "It's just that with celiac disease he gets so sick if he eats anything with gluten in it."

"No gluten. Don't sweat it. I'll watch him."

"I owe you big time."

"You've done hella stuff for me."

"Can I talk to him?"

"Hey kid, want to talk to your mom?" Nan shouted.

"Hi, I played ball with Nan and her neighbor. He has a dog.

"Who does?"

"The neighbor man. A big yellow dog. He licked me." He laughed.

"The man?"

"The dog. Mommy, you're silly." He giggled. "You said I get a puppy when we move to the farm."

"I said maybe." Every kid should have a dog, an animal to play with, and someone to hug when things get tough. But could she handle the extra cost and responsibility right now with their future up in the air? "We'll see."

"I catched the ball."

She let her shoulders relax and grinned hearing her son so excited.

"I catched it more than once and the dog did too." He yawned loudly.

"Honey, you better get ready for bed. I can hear you're tired. I'll call again tomorrow."

"Okay, but I'm not tired."

"It's still time for bed." According to him, he was never tired. She grinned again. "Good night, baby."

"I'm not a baby."

"Then good night, big guy." She chuckled, but a twinge pinched her heart. Her baby was growing up so fast.

"Night." He hung up.

Thanks to Nan, her son was enjoying his first night without her. But without him nearby, Amy couldn't release her need to hug Bobby.

Suddenly cold, she rubbed her arms and put on the kettle for a cup of tea.

At the kitchen table, she took a sip of the orange-spiced liquid. Then she opened the envelope and held the pale pink stationary, covered with darker pink roses, and read her grandmother's unsteady penmanship.

*Amy, my dearest grandbaby,*

*When you read this, I'll be in a better place. Please don't cry or be sad. Know that I was luckier than most people. I spent my life with the man I loved, living on the land we were both privileged to till.*

*My only regret is that I won't see Bobby grow up to be a man. But with you as his mama, I know he's in good hands and he'll grow into a man we can be proud of.*

Amy sniffed and wiped a tear that threatened to run down her cheek and read the rest of the letter.

*Honey, I know you love your life in the city. You never wanted to live on the farm. I understood that. But I leave the property to you with the hope it will not be a burden. Instead, it will be a gift that frees you from the financial struggle of raising a son alone.*

*I smile thinking of you. As a little girl you brought me and your grandpa so much joy, we beamed at the thought of you. From this day on, I pray you and Bobby are blessed with love and happiness.*

*I go from this earth willingly knowing I will soon be with Grandpa. Remember to smile. And even in hard times, look for the bright side of life and you'll find it.*

*With all my love, Granny*

How could she smile without her grandmother? Careful not to tear it, she folded the letter and was about to place it back, when she felt a lump in the envelope and turned it upside down. Something sparkled when it fell out onto the table. Her Grandmother's sterling silver chain, with the crystal heart on it, glistened in the bright kitchen light. Grandpa had given it to her as a birthday present and afterward, Granny had worn it every day. Whenever she thought of her grandmother, she pictured her with the necklace. Amy picked it up and the sobs she'd held back all day gushed out.

"Are you okay?"

She glanced up to see Wyatt standing in the kitchen doorway, a serious expression spreading across his face.

She wrapped her fingers around the little crystal heart to give her strength. "Fine." She wiped her eyes. "I'm okay."

"Good," he said a little too quickly, clearly uncomfortable with her emotion. "I'll be in the downstairs bedroom."

She watched him disappear.

Her grandmother hadn't mentioned Wyatt in the letter. Why the heck had Granny made him the executor of the estate and given half the property to him? Why?

# CHAPTER 3

**Damn,** it was going to be a scorcher. *Eight in the morning and I'm already sweating.* Wyatt pushed his hair back from his forehead and squinted at his new home, the run-down cottage behind Granny's farmhouse. He shook his head and wondered what made him agree to "babysit" Amy and her kid.

He grunted as he remembered the promise he'd made to Granny. He'd stay nearby and make sure Amy and Bobby were all right. He'd also agreed to make repairs and get the farm ready for sale. The sooner he kept his word, the quicker he could get the hell out of town and back where he belonged.

The judge's words rang in his ears. *I leave half interest in my farm, including all the buildings and land, to Wyatt Cameron.*

That sure as hell took him by surprise. Granny had cleverly tied him to the property until he kept his promise to her. Barely five feet tall and as old as Grandma Moses, the crafty old woman, even after death, had made sure she'd get her way to keep him there at the farm until it was sold.

Maybe he should just sign his half back to Amy and leave. He considered it. Then he remembered Granny on the day before she died. Frail and barely able to speak, her eyes were still strong and focused as she'd held his hand and thanked him, in advance, for the promise he'd vowed to keep. *Shit.*

Even now in the blazing sun, he could feel the cold despair he'd experienced after his mother died. A kid on his own, he'd rebelled against everything. He was heading for a bad end, but he hadn't cared.

If Granny hadn't stepped in and helped him get through the grief and anger, he didn't know where he'd be, probably dead or in jail.

Only one way to pay her back, stay and keep his pact, no matter how awkward and uncomfortable the situation. He'd remain on the property and get it ready for a quick sale. Amy had better be ready for that reality.

Yesterday, he'd seen her long strawberry-blonde hair blowing in the hot wind and noticed her nice ass. At that moment, he'd realized he'd been thinking of her the way Granny had, as a little girl. But in the truck when Amy had adjusted her tank top, he'd seen she was all woman.

Years earlier, he'd laughed at the young red-headed kid with the dark-rimmed eyeglasses who had a crush on him. But at the bus stop her hazel eyes were clear and bright, and unhidden by glasses. She'd looked disappointed when she thought he was Granny's handyman. And when she'd heard he had inherited part of the estate, her eyes had blazed with not only hurt but with anger.

Nevertheless, he wasn't about to explain. He didn't believe in explaining much to anyone and certainly not to a woman he hadn't seen since high school and who meant nothing to him. If Granny wanted her to understand the reason for leaving part of the farm to him, it would be in the letter she wrote to Amy.

As he got closer to the neglected cottage, he saw the graying walls in need of paint, as did the sagging front steps.

Maintenance on the farm was costly and Granny wasn't able to keep it going. Now, he'd do a small number of restorations to freshen the place. Then it would not have to be sold as a "fixer" at a below-market price. Before he left town and went back to the rodeo circuit, he'd set the property up to get the highest price possible.

He'd already approached a company that was in the market for property near their Sacramento cannery. Granny's farm fit the bill. Selling to them could be the easy answer for Amy and Bobby.

Last night, he'd wondered if he should describe the ins and outs of organic farming. Tell Amy what she'd be up against if she had even the minutest idea of staying, drought and voracious worms, not to mention fluctuating apple prices and tons of apples, from all over the world, being dumped on the US market. He could mention the old irrigation system needed updating, but since the farm was going to be sold there was no need to bother her.

With her white porcelain skin protected by the San Francisco fog and untouched by the harsh sun of the California foothills, he imagined her wearing high heels and a tight-fitting business suit to a job in the Financial District of the city. She wasn't a country girl anymore. She was metropolitan all the way. Soon, she'd be back in San Francisco where she belonged.

He yanked open the cottage door. A bare light bulb hung from the ceiling of the living room. Old tack and a weathered saddle sat on a broken-down sofa, the couch's rusted springs stuck out, the stuffing gone. An aged wood floor peeked out from a thick layer of dust. Old cardboard boxes lined the walls, covered in yellowing wallpaper, and the slight fragrance of mildew floated in the stale air.

Granny and Grandpa had started their life together in this cottage. The only people he'd known who stayed together through good and bad times to complete their journey until death parted them.

He pushed up the sleeves of his shirt and started the job of moving out the clutter. He worked his way through the living room to the bedroom. The kitchen didn't matter at this point. He wasn't going to cook much. There were always sandwiches or he could drive into town and eat at Mel's Café.

Hours later, covered in dust and his truck bed half full of stuff ready for the dump, he surveyed the cottage. The living room and bedroom were clear.

Coughing, he went to the main house for a bandana to cover his mouth and nose before he tackled the dusty oak floors. He grabbed a kerchief from the dresser in the downstairs bedroom and headed for the back door.

In the kitchen, Amy, barefooted and dressed in white shorts and a pink sleeveless shirt, stood with her back to him. On her tiptoes, she reached for something on the top shelf of the pantry. Her long curly hair wound its way down her back. His fingers itched to feel the silkiness of it.

He scanned her shapely legs from the slender ankles to her firm thighs and tight gluteus maximus. How would it feel to run his calloused hand up the soft creamy skin to her thigh and beyond?

He shook his head. If he were looking for a woman to spend the night with, she'd be first on the list, but the last thing he wanted was more problems in his life. With a kid, she was full of complications. He never knew a woman who wasn't trouble and a single mother was double the aggravation.

With a grunt, he rushed outside. The back door slammed behind him.

*** 

Amy jumped when the door banged shut. She hadn't heard Wyatt enter the house and he was gone before she could say anything. She glanced out of the window framing a view of the backyard.

Wyatt opened the door to the cottage and entered. She was about to turn away when the cottage door opened again and he came out again carrying a huge cardboard box. He tossed it in his pickup and she noticed the truck bed was full of old torn boxes.

Afterward, he stripped off his shirt and hung it on the porch railing. Sweat glistened on his broad chest. She watched him push his brown hair from his face and drink from the garden hose.

His pecks tightened as he doused his hair with water and then shook his head. The movement sent drops of water flying in the air and dripping down to his six-pack abs.

"Whoa," she whispered, sucked in a breath of air and leaned forward for a better view.

He snatched his shirt from the porch rail and headed for the back door. Just then he looked up. She jumped back from the window. Had he seen her staring?

*Look busy.* She grabbed a towel, dried a bowl and put it in the cupboard and dried a dish too. Why was she so nervous? Okay, so she'd had a crush on him in high school and had spent time daydreaming about his kiss. That was years ago. Now he owned half the farm, but he was still only a handyman.

A note she'd written listing the work Wyatt needed to complete lay on the kitchen table. She picked it up.

"It's going to be a scorcher today. Even the water in the hose is hot," he said as he entered the room. He pulled open the freezer, took out an ice tray, and filled a tall glass with ice and water.

"I've made a list of things that need to be done in the next few days before my son arrives." She held a scrap of paper out to him. "The sooner you get started, the better."

He glanced at it but didn't take the list. Instead, a frown spread across his face.

She read the notes to herself and then said, "I've taken my old room upstairs and the guest room is going to be my son's bedroom. It's next to mine and I think he might feel safe if he's closer to me. Bobby thinks he's a big man, but like I said, he's only four."

Wyatt took a drink of water.

"He's a delicate little boy, born prematurely. When he was a baby, I thought I might lose him." She swallowed hard as she thought of the night he almost died. A shiver ran up her spine and she shook it away.

"Anyway, his room is musty and I thought a fresh coat of paint would help. If you could paint it now. Let me see—" She pushed her hair out of her eyes. "Uh, the hall bathroom could use new floor tiles. Nothing fancy, just simple "stick-down" tiles. The old tiles are cracked and I almost tripped on them last night. I don't want Bobby to fall. The sink faucet leaks. It drove me nuts last night, drip, drip, drip. That's just the beginning of the list. But I'd like the ones I mentioned repaired first." She gulped a breath of air. She was rambling, talking too fast and telling too much, but she couldn't seem to stop.

Wyatt stood silent. His face was devoid of emotion. The muscles of his bare chest flexed and she couldn't take her eyes off him. Why wouldn't he put on his damn shirt?

"Please take a look at the list and tell me if you have any questions. I guess the general store still has paint. If I can get Granny's old Volvo station wagon started, I'll go into town and get the paint while you get the room ready. You'll have to tell me what to buy to stop the drip in the sink. I don't have a clue about plumbing. Or paint as far as that goes." She shrugged and yanked her gaze away from his pecks and up to his eyes.

A bemused expression spread over his face. "You misunderstood." He drank the last of the ice water and set the glass on the counter.

"Misunderstood what?"

"I'm not Granny's handyman."

"But yesterday you said you were."

"I said *you* could call me that. If I didn't, you weren't going to get in the truck. Everyone was waiting for you at the courthouse."

"But you said and I thought…"

"I helped your grandmother because she didn't have anyone else and she let me use her barn to store my equipment. That's all."

"Uh—"

26

"Look, Amy, I'll get the room ready for your kid and take care of the tile and the drip in the bathroom. And a few other things that need to be done around here. I promised Granny I'd help you. But you have to work too. Deal?"

"Uh, yeah. Deal."

"Good." He pulled his cotton shirt over his head and down his chest, covering his physique.

"Thank you."

"For what?"

She wanted to say, for covering your distracting body, but instead, she cleared her throat. "For promising to help me."

"Besides getting your kid's room ready, you better line up someone to harvest the apples. Granny usually called Manuel Gordon and his crew. They're popular and get grabbed up fast. And they may not have time, but they're the best. His phone number must be around here somewhere or I have it. It needs to be done before you sell the farm."

"Uh—about that. I planned to put the place on the market, but now that I'm here—" Seeing his expression, she hesitated.

"This morning, I walked in the apple orchards." Eager to make him understand, she continued. "I felt the soil between my fingers and smelled the apples still on the trees. I picked one. I'd forgotten what it tasted like right off the branch. When I bit into it, the juice ran down my chin." She grinned. "I was a kid again eating fruit for the first time. It was awesome. Suddenly, Granny was there, standing next to me, telling me to keep and run the farm."

He rolled his eyes and she noted his Amy-is-a-crazy-person expression.

She stepped closer. "Wyatt, I'm not insane. Of course, I know Granny wasn't there. Yet, I've seen her walk the orchards so many times, it was as if her essence was next to me, saying this farm is my home. I haven't felt like I belong anywhere since I left Sierra Creek. Can you understand that?"

Before he could answer, she said, "For the first time in my adult life, I'm truly a part of something—the land. And for the first time, I understood the meaning of the word home."

She crossed her arms and moved only steps from him. "The farm is Bobby's heritage and I'll do whatever I can to nurture and protect his legacy."

"All by yourself?"

"Yeah."

She noted the skepticism in his features as his eyes narrowed.

"To honor my grandmother, I'm calling the company Granny's Organic Apples."

"It's easy to name a business, but running a farm is hard, dirty work. I see your pale skin and perfectly manicured fingernails. What job did you have in San Francisco?"

She quickly put her hands behind her back.

"Well?"

"I was a bank teller until they closed the branch and replaced it with an ATM. I want a job that can't be outsourced or offshored. I have a chance to do something that matters, give people organic food. They won't have to worry about pesticides in the apples and juice they feed their kids. You can't have any idea what it means to a mother to watch her baby eat and drink knowing the apples are free of poison."

She held up her hand to stop him from speaking. "Okay, so maybe I'll never be rich—money rich. But if Bobby and I can spend our days taking care of the farm and feeding people poison-free food, then no matter what our bank account says, we're rich."

"Enough." His eyes narrowed. "I understand all that warm and fuzzy, save and feed the earth crap. I wish things were that clear. People with good ideas and great results. Things aren't." He glared at her. "Try and save the planet when you can't feed your kid, and aren't able to pay your bills."

"Who hurt you? How did you get so cynical?"

He flinched. "This isn't about me. It's about you and your kid. What do you know about working on a farm?"

"Well—uh." She looked away, grabbed a dish towel, and twisted it in her hands. "I—" She finally met his stare. "Nothing. I don't know anything about running a farm."

"Really?" His right eyebrow rose as he stared at her. "What would you say if I told you your grandmother wanted you to sell? In fact, she told me to get rid of it for you?"

"I wouldn't believe you. Granny loved this place. She'd never want me to sell."

"She knew you and remembered how you high-tailed it off the farm and out of Sierra Creek to live in San Francisco as soon as you were old enough to get away. Granny told me your last words to her were 'I hate this place and I'm never coming back.'"

He ran his hand over his chin. "You have no idea how much your words hurt her."

"That's not fair. I was a teenager. I didn't understand what Granny had. What I had."

"How often have you visited since you left? Once a year? At Christmas time? Did you ever ask how the farming business was doing? Or if she needed your help?"

"I—"

"These last few years Granny needed you, wanted your help, Amy. But she'd never ask. And you were too busy with your own life to care. You weren't here for her then. Don't keep the place out of regret now. It won't do her any good. Soothe your guilt some other way."

"How dare you?" She reeled from the shock of his words. "What do you know anyway?"

"More than you think."

She winced, recalling her struggle in the last few years to feed her son and pay the rent, especially after her no-good husband took the little money she had, and walked out. All he'd left her to remember him by was the swollen lip he'd given her and the huge bill he'd run up on her credit card. Even so, Wyatt was right. That was no excuse. She should have helped Granny.

Deep in her thoughts, she jumped when Wyatt cleared his throat.

"I'm not going to argue with you." She squared her shoulders and glared at him. "I'm a quick study. When I make up my mind to do something, I do it. No one can stop me."

She threw the dish towel on the kitchen table and tried to hold her tongue. Unsuccessful, she spat the words, "Wyatt, I'm going to keep and run Granny's farm. I will succeed. So, help me or get the hell out of my way."

# CHAPTER 4

**Amy** regretted her words as soon as she saw Wyatt's expression harden. It caused a shudder to run through her. She looked away. Why hadn't she kept quiet instead of shooting off her big mouth? But she had a habit of saying more than she should when people riled her. With a quick breath, she glanced at him. He hadn't moved a muscle and continued to stare at her.

After her grand declaration, he still had control of half of the farm and she needed his help if the place was going to be a successful working farm.

*Better change the subject.* "I'd still like you to help me get the house ready for my son." Her voice sounded tentative even to her ears.

He grunted and then said, "Let me take a look at the sink in the bathroom. Then I'll go with you to get the plumbing and the paint."

"Uh good—fine."

He left the room.

She exhaled and leaned against the kitchen table. She'd told Wyatt she'd succeed because nothing could stop her, but her body trembled with insecurity. If she failed, she was risking her future. More importantly, she was gambling with Bobby's legacy.

**\*\*\***

Later that day, back from the store and in what would be her son's bedroom, Amy slowly turned and scanned the walls for spots that might need a touch of blue paint.

Wyatt had been right about the color. The pale sky-blue walls were soothing yet masculine enough for a young boy. Bobby would love them. The navy plaid bedding he owned would look terrific in the room.

She'd never painted before, hadn't ever bought a can of paint until today, and would have taken forever trying to decide what to buy. Matte, eggshell, gloss, it was a foreign language to her, but Wyatt had taken it all in stride.

There was only one area left to paint. She rubbed her arm. Yeah, it was sore, but the room was almost finished and she was burning calories. She smiled, dipped her roller into the paint, and tackled the last wall.

Wyatt was working next door in the bathroom. She recalled how he had, with little effort, found everything they needed in the plumbing department. He'd even chosen black and white self-stick tiles for the room, a perfect choice for the old farmhouse.

She entered the washroom holding the paint-covered roller and stared at the floor. "Wow! I can't believe the difference the new tiles make. The bathroom's beautiful."

"You better clean that roller or the paint will dry on it and you'll have to buy a new one."

"Oh." She carried it to the sink, careful not to drop paint on the new floor. After scrubbing the roller, she turned off the water. "The sink doesn't drip anymore."

"Easy to fix."

"Maybe for you, but I couldn't do it—thanks." She surveyed the rest of the room. "I'd forgotten the tub is so big. The bathroom in my old apartment was so tiny and it only had room for a small shower. Bobby's going to love the claw-footed tub."

"You'll have to buy him a rubber duck." He grinned.

Her body warmed when she saw his smile. "You're right."

"That should do it." He slid the final tile into place, stood, and brushed off his jeans.

"I can't thank you enough. It's gorgeous."

"No big deal. Clean up and I'll buy you dinner."

"I owe you a home-cooked meal after all the work you've done. But I haven't gone to the grocery store yet. Will you take a rain check?"

"Don't worry about it." He leaned forward and brushed a strand of hair out of her face. "Get the paint out of your hair and we'll go."

So close to him, she closed her eyes believing he was going to kiss her.

"Meet me downstairs. I'll give you thirty minutes to clean up." He stepped away and began to pick up his tools.

Even after all the things he'd said about the way she treated Granny and her angry response, she wanted to go to dinner with him. Did the crush she'd had on him in high school still linger today?

\*\*\*

What the hell was he thinking, asking Amy to dinner? He hadn't meant to ask her. Sexy, with disheveled hair, and pouty lips, she'd stared at him with her huge hazel eyes and the invitation had just popped out of him.

She was attractive, but that's not what drew him to her. He'd seen lots of beautiful women, fashionable ones who were better dressed, more put together than Amy. Many sexy women followed the rodeo circuit looking for a champion cowboy with prize money to spend on a lady and a good time. But they wouldn't get their hands dirty or care about putting manicured fingers on a paintbrush to make a room just right for their kid. Amy had put her son's needs before her own. The room she was using certainly needed paint more than Bobby's room did. Still, she ignored that fact and painted her son's room first. That intrigued him.

He grunted. He had no interest in a relationship. Keeping his promise to Granny and getting back on the rodeo circuit was his goal. He better not lose sight of that fact. Still, he smiled with satisfaction at the thought of Amy's son enjoying his newly painted room. Every child should have a place of their own. As a kid, after his parents divorced, he'd wanted his own space but never got one. His mother's living room couch was as close as he got to a room of his own.

***

Twenty minutes later, Amy, dressed in a yellow cotton sundress, was in the living room ready to go when her smartphone rang. She quickly yanked it from her small shoulder bag. "Hello."

"Mommy, come home," Bobby sobbed.

"Baby, what's wrong? Why are you crying?"

"I fell down."

"Oh, baby. Are you hurt?"

"Mommy, I want you."

"Honey."

"Come back."

"Let me talk to Nan."

"Okay." He sniffed.

"Amy?"

"Nan, what happened?" Amy tried to control the panic in her voice. "Is he okay?" She spoke more quietly and then took a quick breath to slow her breathing and glanced up to see a look of concern tighten Wyatt's features.

"Bobby's fine. He tripped over the neighbor's dog and scraped his chin. I put antibiotic cream and a band-aid on it. Don't worry. He's okay."

"Thank God. I was so worried. I should be with him. He sounds so upset. You're sure he's all right? I should've taken him with me. I didn't know what I'd find up here and I had to get the place ready and—"

"Calm down. He just misses you, but he's good. I think the fall scared him more than anything else. I'd be the first to tell you if he was seriously hurt."

"I know. I just feel so guilty for not being there. If I had a car I could drive back."

"Even if you did, by the time you got to my place it'd be midnight. Bobby would be asleep."

"You're right." Could she ask Wyatt to drive her to San Francisco? She glanced at him. After she told him to get out of her way, he'd spent the day helping her. It'd be pushing it to ask him to do more tonight.

"Look, Amy, I'd drive Bobby to the farm now, but my car is being repaired. It'll be ready in a couple of days. I'll bring Bobby to the farm as soon as I pick up my car from the repair shop. Okay?"

"Yeah, that's fine. Can I talk to Bobby again?"

"Sure."

"Mommy.

"You okay?"

"Yeah." He sniffed again.

"Honey, I can't see you tonight. I need you to be a big boy and stay with Nan. Okay?"

"Yeah."

Her heart clenched. "You can watch a movie and then go to bed."

"Lady and the Tramp?" he asked eagerly.

"Okay and then go straight to bed."

"Love you, Mommy."

"I love you too—big guy." She remembered not to call him a baby, though the name came naturally to her lips.

Her heart pounded and her hand shook when she disconnected the phone.

"Is your boy all right?" Wyatt frowned.

"Yeah. Just a scratched chin—thank goodness. But it scared me. He's been sick and he's so delicate." She forced an imitation of a smile. "It's hard to be away from him even for a little while."

"That's natural." Wyatt moved toward her. "You love him."

"More than life itself." Her words echoed loudly in the quiet farmhouse.

Wyatt's intense eyes widened. "I bet."

He seemed to understand. That surprised her.

An awkward silence surrounded them as she considered what to say next. She leaned toward him and could feel heat radiating from him.

With his large hand, he reached out to touch her cheek and she let him. It was rough, yet gentle at the same time. She noted how truly deep blue his eyes were. Too bad she couldn't decipher the emotions behind them.

He cleared his throat and stepped back. "You'd probably like to be at home if Bobby calls again. That way you can relax and you won't have to worry about hearing your cell in a loud restaurant. We can go to dinner another night?" He paused. "What say I order ravioli dinners to go and bring them back here?"

His words broke into her thoughts as if he'd read her mind. Did he want to get away from an over-emotional single mother or did he truly know what she was going through? She gazed at him, unable to decide the truth.

"Thanks. I'd like that." Her cell phone rang again. She answered it and when she looked up, Wyatt was gone.

# CHAPTER 5

**Two** days had passed since Wyatt brought the ravioli dinners to the farm. They'd eaten in the living room in front of a fire burning in the fireplace and passed the time as old friends talking about high school. The conversation had been easy. A feeling of closeness had churned in her. The sense that she'd reconnected with a dear friend. Even though she'd hardly known him in high school because he was a senior when she was a freshman.

The following morning she'd looked out of her bedroom window and his truck was gone from the driveway. Now forty-eight hours later, she hadn't seen or heard from him. Fear that he wouldn't return rippled through her, tightening her back muscles.

Without his phone number, she couldn't call or text. Anyway, if he didn't want to be there helping her, she wasn't going to beg him. But damn, he owned half the farm. He should do half the work to repair the place. Her hands fisted. He didn't deserve any of Bobby's legacy.

Enough, she couldn't change the will, but she was in charge of the farm now. Right? Too bad she didn't know what the hell she should do to fix the place.

Her head throbbed. She rubbed the tension from her forehead. *All I need is a migraine.* With closed eyes, she took a slow breath. No matter how she felt, it was time to get to work.

Manuel Gordon's phone number was in Granny's old rolltop desk in the den. She called to arrange for the harvesting of the apples and found Wyatt had already contacted him and made a date. Was that his parting "good deed" before leaving her to run the place?

Her angry tirade telling Wyatt to help or get the hell out of the way flashed in her memory. She groaned. Too many times in her life she'd spit out angry words before she could think better of it. Like telling Granny she hated the farm and was never coming back. That was certainly biting her in the ass right now. Other times her speech had gotten her in trouble. She should've learned by now, but no she'd done it again.

"Shit."

Later, she drove Granny's old Volvo station wagon to the curb in front of Sophie's Ice Cream Parlor on Main Street, yanked on the brake, and turned off the engine. "Ice Cream", the flamboyant red sign stated. But like Sophie herself, it had faded a little but was still one of the brightest banners on the main street.

After working on the farm and expending a lot of calories in the last few days, Amy could eat an ice cream sundae without guilt, and as Granny's best friend, maybe Sophie had answers to the questions that still bugged Amy. If Sophie knew, would she tell her?

The glass front door opened and she heard the familiar tinkle of the little bell attached to it.

Today, the huge ice cream parlor was empty. Still, the strong aroma of freshly made ice cream permeated the room and caused her mouth to water. The smell of the vanilla ice cream mingled nicely with the scent of peppermint and chocolate candy.

She gazed around the well-known room. Photos of milkshakes, banana splits, and sodas hung on the deep pink walls. Though now a little worn, heart-shaped metal-backed chairs with red leather seats sat in the same formation around the metal tables as they had twenty years earlier. As a six-year-old child, she'd come here to eat her first ice cream sundae.

Sophie stood behind the counter. A heavy-set, gray-haired woman wearing a white apron spotted with strawberry ice cream smears. It was stretched over the plus-size tan dress she wore. Except for her graying hair, she appeared as she had on the first day Amy had met her.

The woman rushed to her and pulled her into a tight hug. "Amy, honey, I'm so sorry about your grandmother—but it's good to see you again."

"It's wonderful to see you too." She hugged the woman back. Childhood memories of eating Rocky Road ice cream in the shop flashed.

"Granny mentioned you in her will. I'll bring the Windsor rocking chair and the grandfather clock she wanted you to have."

"Oh—it's just like your Granny to give away something that was admired. She was a wonderful woman, always giving to others, and never worrying about her own needs. There are too few people like that in the world." Sophie wiped tears from her eyes.

Amy hugged the woman again and smiled. "Granny wanted you to have them." She cleared her throat. "How's Vanna?" A memory of playing with Sophie's daughter filled her.

"She's fine. Moved back," Sophie said. "I told her you were going to be here. She's coming to the shop—should be here pretty soon."

"Great. We have a lot of catching up to do."

"I'll get you a sundae. You still want Rocky Road ice cream in yours just like you used to?"

Amy grinned, feeling like a little girl again. "Yep. It's the best."

Sophie laughed. "It's Vanna's favorite too."

Amy sat at the table by the window. "Vanna and I used to sit at this table and hope a cute boy would see us and come in and join us. We were so naïve."

Sophie set the biggest Sundae she'd ever seen on the table in front of her and then joined her at the table. "Dig in."

She took a bite as Sophie watched.

"Mm, you make the best ice cream in the world. I've missed it. The cartons of frozen stuff in the supermarkets aren't any good, not since I've tasted your ice cream. You spoiled me." She wiped her chin to catch a drip of chocolate sauce.

"Thanks, Amy."

"The place is quiet today."

"Yeah. Business is down since the mill closed, and these days everybody's so careful about spending their money and, on top of that, they're worrying about eatin too much, calories, cholesterol and all." She shrugged. "I've been thinking what to do to bring in more customers, and give the teenagers in town somewhere to go."

"There must be something. Your ice cream is so worth the calories." Amy ate another spoonful of Rocky Road.

"Vanna thinks I should add coffee drinks like the ones in the new coffee shops that have opened all over Sacramento. You know places with lattes and fancy teas." Sophie shrugged.

"That's a great idea."

"I guess. It might be time to update the old place," Sophie agreed, but her voice was touched with sadness.

"Keep the ice cream too. I want Bobby to grow up knowing what real ice cream tastes like."

"I feel better just hearing you say that." The woman smiled. "Is everything going okay on the farm?"

"Yeah, it's all good. I painted a room for Bobby. He's excited about coming up here."

"And how are you and Wyatt gettin on?"

"Fine, fine," she said a little too quickly, looked away from Sophie, and forced ice cream down her tightened throat.

"Really?"

"No." Amy sighed. "I told him I wasn't going to sell. I yelled at him to get the hell out of my way. I swore I was going to run the farm myself." She swallowed marshmallow sauce and it stuck in her throat. She coughed. "I haven't seen Wyatt for two days. He's probably done with me." She pushed the ice cream sundae away, her appetite gone. "He hates me."

"Amy, I'm sure he doesn't."

"He does. Now, I don't even have a handyman to get things ready, if I did want to sell—which I don't. Oh hell, I'm not making a lot of sense."

"He'll be back. He promised Granny he'd help you and he's not a man to go back on his word." She patted Amy's hand. "You two are under a big strain with your Granny dying. That's all."

"I guess you're right. I miss her so much." Amy gulped back a sob. "I wish I hadn't yelled at him." She tried to eat her melting sundae but couldn't.

"Amy, I should tell you something about Wyatt."

"What's that?"

"He's not a handyman. He's a five-time all-around champion rodeo rider. He's got the gold buckles and a big bank account to prove it. He even makes TV commercials selling boots, hats, and stuff with his name on them. A real celebrity, he's got women all over the country wanting to marry him. Of course, he's not the marrying kind."

Amy's spoon stopped, suspended midway to her open mouth. A drop of the white sticky stuff dropped into her lap. She tossed the spoon back into the dish. "But—Wyatt lives on Granny's farm and works fixing up the place." She scrubbed the spot of marshmallow sauce on her clothes with her napkin. "Why didn't he tell me?"

"Men don't talk much and never talk about their feelings. You know that."

"Sophie, I don't know anything. I'm so terrible at understanding men. Not enough experience at it, I guess. The only man I picked was the wrong one."

"Well, Wyatt's okay. He helped your Granny because he loved her like the grandmother he never had. What could he say to you? Look at me. I'm an important rich rodeo star?" Sophie giggled. "I'm sorry to laugh, but you should see the shocked expression on your face."

"I feel so stupid. I was sorry for him. I thought he needed money. I almost gave him a tip for helping me." She slapped her face. "Oh, God, I'm glad I didn't do that. I'm so embarrassed."

"Amy, it's my fault. I should've told you. But he's such a celebrity in town I thought you'd realize."

"I could've asked him what he'd been doing. I just decided I knew he was the money-grubbing handyman." She cringed. "All I could think about was my situation. Never bothered to ask him anything. Sometimes, I can be so self-centered."

"Don't be so hard on yourself. With your divorce, losing your job, and then worrying about Bobby's health, and Granny dying, you've been through a tough time. Certainly, you're concerned about your situation."

"I can't understand why Granny would give half the farm to Wyatt. I thought she loved me."

"You know she did. More than you can understand."

"Then why? I'm her only grandchild. He's not even a distant cousin. He's not family. He's nothing."

"Uh— well, I guess you could say she owed him." Sophie wiped her hands on her apron and looked away.

"What could she owe him that was worth half the farm?"

Sophie took a deep breath and wiped her hands on her apron again as if she needed something to do to hold off answering the question.

44

"When you were living in the city, your grandpa got sick, terrible sick. Granny took him to the doctors, but after a time there was nothing more the docs could do for Grandpa. It was awful for your grandma." Sophie paused and shook her head. "Real bad." She hesitated. "The hospital administrator said Grandpa had to move out since there was no more the hospital could do for him. They needed Grandpa's bed for patients they could help."

Tears filled Sophie's eyes and she dabbed them with her apron. "He was too ill for Granny to care for him at home. He had to go to hospice." She paused. "That's real expensive, you know, that hospice care. We all wanted to help, but what could we do? With all of us only scraping by."

The woman adjusted her considerable weight in the metal chair and breathed heavily as if the memory was almost too much for her to relive.

With the solitary sound of an old regulator clock to mark the passing of time, Amy waited for Sophie to continue.

When she didn't speak, Amy said, "I should have realized. Should have done something." She caught the woman's eye. "Why didn't Granny tell me?"

"Heck, your grandma knew you didn't have any money. You were like the rest of us barely gettin by. She didn't want you alarmed. You had enough to worry about with Bobby being sick. Any money you had needed to go for his care."

"But that doesn't tell me why Granny thought she owed Wyatt."

Sophie spit out a sigh. "Well, you see—he was doing real good on the rodeo circuit. When he heard about your grandpa needing help, he just up and paid for the hospice care. Wouldn't listen to nobody. He just signed a check and that was that."

Amy gasped. "I'm shocked. Why would he pay Grandpa's bill?"

"Guess he had his reasons. You know, after his mama died, he was a wild teen nobody wanted. Wyatt's dad didn't want a kid reminding him of the woman he'd just divorced. So, he left Wyatt to manage on his own."

Sophie stopped and gazed out the window, her tense expression pulling her lips into a thin line and her eyes narrowed in sadness. "An angry teen, Wyatt was heading for no good. Probably be in jail by now if Granny hadn't stepped in and helped him. So, when she needed money for Grandpa, Wyatt paid." Sophie stared at her. "Honey, I got to tell you when that cowboy makes up his mind to do something, isn't nobody going to change it."

The woman pushed a stray hair out of her face and forced it back under the hairnet she wore. "Your grandma never forgot what Wyatt did for your granddad. She wasn't the type of woman to go to "her maker" without she paid her debts first."

"But..." Amy tried to interrupt.

"She gave the only thing of value she had, half the farm. I knew what she'd done, but she swore me to secrecy. She didn't tell you or Wyatt. I imagine he was as surprised as you when he heard it at the reading of the will."

"I'm stunned."

The doorbell jingled and two teenagers dressed in jeans and t-shirts walked into the ice cream parlor.

"I'll be right back." Sophie hurried from the table.

"Kids, what can I get you?" Sophie asked.

"We want two cones, one double scoop of chocolate on a sugar cone and one scoop of strawberry on a regular cone."

Amy pushed back the new information about Wyatt, too much to digest. Instead, she glanced at the teens. *Nothing much for them to do here in the summer or the winter, for that matter.* She remembered how bored she had been, so ready to get out of town and go to the big city.

Outside the window, the town's people strolled by. She watched and recognized a few faces. Years earlier, she could have named everyone. On the streets of San Francisco, she'd usually seen only strangers in the crowds.

In Sierra Creek, the people waved to each other and stopped to chat. There seemed to be no rush. It was as if the clock moved slower here, time enough to enjoy each moment.

The little bell on the front door sounded again and Amy glanced up expecting to see the teens leave. Vanna, her friend and Sophie's daughter rushed through the door. Her long blonde hair pulled into a ponytail, her beautiful face devoid of makeup, blue eyes glistening, she waved to her mother. "Mom, is Amy here yet?"

Before Sophie could answer, Amy shouted and jumped up to greet Vanna with a hug. "Hey."

"Hey yourself, Amy."

"I'll make you a sundae just like the one I made for Amy," Sophie shouted, a metal ice cream scoop in her hand.

"Just a diet coke, Mom. Thanks."

"Still watching your weight? You're fine. You should eat something."

"I know Mom, but if I don't watch my weight, no man will want to watch me." She winked.

"You look great." Amy smiled. "When I was in San Francisco, I saw you on TV in a shampoo commercial."

"My one claim to fame." Vanna wrinkled her nose and laughed. "So, Amy, how was the city?"

Sophie brought a glass of cola to the table and then left to wait on a new customer.

"I love San Francisco. It's beautiful. A great place to visit, but it's awfully expensive to live there. And I learned there's too much country left in me to live in any city. I missed all the things I thought I wanted to escape, open spaces, blue skies and hot nights and hotter days, even nosy people who know your business."

Amy took a spoon of the melted ice cream and savored the chocolate flavor. "I'm so tired of busy people who won't give you the time of day if you can't do something for them first. They won't take the time to get to know you and are always looking for an angle. Sorry, if I sound bitter. I don't mean to. Never mind. Like I said, I'm tired."

"Listen, Amy, I just came from the wilds of Los Angeles, with its freeways and second-stage smog alerts, and millions of people clogging the streets. Everybody's rushing to make a buck so they can afford to stay in LA instead of going back home to some Podunk town. I'm with you. I was never so glad to beat a retreat home."

They both laughed.

"You're so talented you should be a star in Hollywood."

"Yeah, I was going to set the world of show business on fire." Vanna took a sip of coke. "All I got was a Los Angeles sunburn. Oh, and I discovered I was no different than the ten thousand other blondes from all over the country that came by bus, plane, and train to make it big in Hollywood." She laughed without humor.

"But you're beautiful too."

"Thanks. It's hard to have an ego when you're in a room full of beautiful women just as talented as you are. And every year they seemed to be younger, taller, and thinner than I am."

She finished her cola. "Anyway, I got sick of the smog, traffic, and crowds. Too much country in me too, I guess." Vanna smiled. "I didn't much care what my clothes cost, or if they were made by the latest "fad" designer. I didn't yearn to own an imported sports car or live in Bel Air or Malibu. I woke up one day and realized I didn't much care about anything anymore. That's when I knew it was time to come home." Vanna glanced out the window.

"Well, here we are sitting in the same chairs at the same table in your mom's shop. I guess we've come full circle." She held up her empty sundae glass and tapped Vanna's glass of Diet Coke. "Here's to us and a new start back in our old hometown."

They both laughed.

"It's so good to see you, Vanna."

"Same here—darn good."

***

Amy stayed at the ice cream parlor until Vanna had to return to work at the local daycare center at the Methodist Church.

As the director of the program, Vanna had promised there was space for Bobby. That was a great relief because, until that moment, she hadn't been sure how she'd have time to run the farm and give Bobby the care and entertainment he needed and still earn enough money to pay the bills.

On the way home, she stopped at the grocery store to pick up a few things for the next couple of days. She was at the checkout stand, to pay for her food, when she looked up and saw Mike Donnelly walking toward her.

In high school, everyone called him "Big Mike." Not because he was so big, though he was six feet tall. It was because his younger cousin was called "Little Mike," though he was six feet tall too.

"Hey, Amy."

"Hi, Mike."

"I heard you were back."

"Yeah, just got here. You're the manager, right?"

"Yep, for a couple of years now. I'll help you out to your car."

"Thanks."

He carried her groceries to the wagon and put them in the back of the old Volvo.

"Well—nice to see you, Amy. You're looking good."

"Thanks, Mike." She got into the driver's side of the car.

"See you around."

"Yeah." She waved goodbye. Big Mike had grown into a handsome guy with wavy blonde hair, hazel eyes, and an easy grin. Unlike Wyatt, there was nothing brooding about him. He was as open and friendly as she remembered from high school.

On the way out of town, she stopped at Andy's General Store and picked up a couple of puzzles and a coloring book with farm animals inside, a welcome-to-your-new-home gift for Bobby.

She'd hoped Wyatt's truck would be there when she drove into the driveway of the old farmhouse. No luck. She'd better face the fact he wasn't coming back to help her.

She parked the car near the barn and locked the driver's side door. Wyatt had use of the barn, but she still owned it. She had the right to enter and see if there was anything of value in the old building.

It had been years since she'd been in there. With a yank on the barn door, she dragged it open. The large room smelled of hay and horses. A breeze blew through the door, unsettling the dust, and she sneezed. It took a second for her eyes to adjust to the dim light. The horse stalls were empty, but new hay filled the loft. She grimaced recalling the day she'd jumped off the loft and nearly landed on a pointed pitchfork covered in hay.

In the back corner of the room, equipment loomed casting dark shadows. From where she stood, she couldn't make out the apparatus. As she slowly walked toward it her foot kicked something and glanced down to see the floor was covered with black rubber matting.

A string hung from the rafters. She pulled it. A fluorescent light sputtered and blinked on, lighting a full state-of-the-art workout room with a stationary bike, treadmill, elliptical, free weights and a bench and more, Wyatt's gear. He must have spent a lot of money on this setup. Where the hell was he? Was it any of her business?

# CHAPTER 6

**The** sun sent a jab of daylight through the bare window and woke Wyatt. He threw off the cotton blanket and sat up on the sofa in his brother's one-bedroom apartment in Sacramento. With a deep breath, he stretched the crick out of his back. Then wrinkled his nose and glanced at the open-plan kitchen piled high with dirty dishes, old pizza boxes, and empty beer bottles. Hot air blowing in from the open kitchen window didn't do much to mitigate the smell.

Where did Wes keep the coffee? Wyatt rummaged through the cupboards. A bag of ground Italian roast beans and the French coffee press sat in the corner of the bottom shelf.

Slowly, the aroma of hot coffee began to replace the stale odor in the room.

For no reason he could understand, an image of Amy stretched out in front of the fireplace, her eyes warm, and her full lips smiling at him flashed in his memory. His body tightened. The thought of touching her, kissing her, increased his temperature. She probably wondered where he was and why he had disappeared after they ate dinner together.

He could have told her he was leaving to visit his brother. However, explaining his movements wasn't something that came easily. After spending the evening together, he'd felt something for Amy. He wasn't about to figure out what and he'd seen desire in her eyes as she smiled at him. It would have been easy to stay and get even closer. She wasn't a virgin after all.

He shook his head. It was better he left for a couple of days and got his mind back on track and his head on straight. He'd concentrate on healing and get back on the rodeo circuit. That's all he needed in his life right now.

Wes came into the living room wearing only his boxers. He ran his hands through his short brown hair. Wyatt smiled. His little brother had grown. Damn if he wasn't almost as tall as his own six-foot height.

"I didn't think you'd still be here." Wes yawned. "I don't want to be inhospitable, but I've got plans and they don't include an older brother hanging around the living room. If you get my drift."

"Subtlety isn't your strong suit, bro. Don't worry. I'll be out before your woman gets here." Wyatt laughed and then wrinkled his nose as the heat of the day increased the smell of flat beer and stale food. "If I were you, I'd get rid of the beer bottles and air out the place before she lands on your doorstep."

"Don't need to. My gal loves the real me and I don't want to spoil her. She enjoys cleaning up after me."

"You're a pig."

"Yeah, but women think I'm hot." Wes grinned.

Wyatt couldn't help but smile too. His younger brother was twenty-seven going on eighteen. Was he ever that cocky?

"I'm going to take a shower. I made coffee, Wes. But don't drink it all. I want another cup."

When he came back into the living room, his younger brother was dressed in jeans and was pulling on a white t-shirt, but still no shoes. But the pizza boxes and the beer bottles were gone. Though the dirty dishes were still piled high, maybe there was hope for Wes after all.

To glance at his brother, Wyatt turned quickly, felt a shooting pain in his back, and grimaced again.

"Hey, how's your back?" Wes asked. "Guess sleeping on my couch didn't do it any good."

"I'm fine."

"Wyatt, when are you going back on the circuit? It's no fun unless I have someone good to beat."

"Win against me? Only in your dreams, little brother. Enjoy it without me, because when I come back, I'll kick your ass." Wyatt laughed.

"Yeah, right," Wes smirked. "Bring it on anytime, I'm ready."

Wyatt went to the kitchen and poured a cup of coffee, then sat at the kitchen table. Dressed in blue jeans, he buttoned the blue chambray shirt, tucked it in, and bent down to pull on his boots. Just the action of reaching for his boots sent pain into his back and right shoulder. He groaned and looked up to see if his brother had noticed. Wes didn't need to know how badly hurt he was. No one did.

He'd ignored his injury until the pain had finally forced him to see a doctor. The doctor told him he was lucky to still have a full range of motion. His right shoulder could have frozen up.

The medic had given him specific exercises to strengthen his back and shoulder and written him a prescription to dull the ache. How much time and exercise would he have to endure before the doctor told him he could get back on a horse? When would he be cleared to compete again?

He had to exercise every day, but his equipment sat in Granny's barn. How was he going to use it? Damn, he didn't want to see Amy right now.

"I'll scramble some eggs for us and then you need to get out of here." Wes's voice broke into his thoughts.

"Yeah, okay."

"Wyatt."

"Yep."

"I'm glad you came by. I don't see enough of you these days."

"Then come up to the farm and visit. It looks like I'm going to be stuck there for a while."

\*\*\*

The sun was setting when Wyatt drove the Ford F150 into the driveway of Granny's farm. He parked next to the old Volvo.

At the sound of his truck, he thought Amy might look out the window. When she didn't leave the house, he took his groceries and went into the cottage, relieved he didn't have to make small talk with her.

After tossing the food in the cupboard, he went to the barn to work out and get rid of the excess adrenaline pumping through his veins.

\*\*\*

The berry patch was larger than Amy remembered. Granny had taken the berries to the health food store every year. She would do the same. A little extra money was dearly needed.

She'd been in the patch since eight in the morning
and found it took longer to get the fruit ready for
market than she'd thought. As she wiped the sweat
from her brow, Granny's worn straw hat slipped off
her head. She grabbed it before it hit the ground and
plopped it back on her head. How many times had
she seen her grandmother working in the patch
wearing the old-fashioned Panama?

Amy gazed up at the sun. It had to be past noon.
The hottest time of the day was still ahead of her. She
wiped her brow again, took a deep breath, and wished
she had a cold drink.

The raspberry and blackberry bushes were
bursting with fruit. A great crop if they got to the
store in time. While she was working in San
Francisco, raspberries had been out of her budget.
They were her favorite berry, but she didn't buy them.
Her son had never had one. He was in for a real treat.
She smiled and set aside a couple of small boxes for
him, and popped one of the organic raspberries in her
mouth. Her taste buds sprang to life and she moaned
with pleasure.

This morning she'd called Tom, the owner of the
health food store. He was happy to have the fruit, but
the berries had a short shelf life. She needed to get
them to the store before it closed today. She'd have to
put the fruit in the Volvo and be ready to go soon.
She stretched and went back to selecting the best
berries, not too green and not over ripe.

Manuel and his crew would pick the apples soon.
With the money from the apples and the berries, she
hoped there'd be enough to get through the next
couple of months. While she lived on that money,
she'd tend to Granny's pumpkin patch and Christmas

trees. The cash from those crops would keep them going.

"Ouch." She pricked her finger and automatically brought it to her mouth and sucked on it.

With her hands held out in front of her, she glared at her fruit-stained fingers and broken fingernails. So much for the manicure she'd splurged on, just before she'd left San Francisco. Then she noticed a drip of blood on her hand and saw several scratches. *Damn. The berries are fighting back.* She smiled at the thought.

One more row of berries and she'd be done. As a kid, it had been such fun to help Granny in the berry patch. But then she'd eaten as much fruit as she picked. When it got hot or she got tired, she walked away leaving her grandmother to finish the job.

Finally, the berries were lugged to the car and set into the back of the Volvo wagon, she glanced at the old wristwatch that belonged to her granddad. Just enough time to get the fruit to the store before it shut for the night.

She dug out the car key from her cutoff jeans, jumped into the driver's seat, and tried to start the engine. It made a grinding sound, but it wouldn't turnover. When she tried again, it didn't even groan, it only clicked.

"If you keep pumping the gas, you're going to flood that old engine."

She jumped when she heard Wyatt's deep voice. She hadn't noticed him come out of the cottage and stand next to the driver's side door. Grateful, she pushed back questions about where he'd been for the last couple of days. None of her business, he owed her no explanation. She had to remember that, even though she was curious.

"I have to take the berries to Tom's store before it closes."

"Let me try to start the car."

She slid to the passenger's seat.

When he turned the key, she heard the click, then nothing.

"Did you leave the lights on last night?"

*Don't be stupid. Of course, I didn't leave the lights on.* She swallowed her first thought. "The lights were off when I parked last night. When I first started to drive, my grandmother told me to always check the headlights before I left the car. I never forgot that.

"Okay. I'll take a look under the hood."

Amy wandered back and forth next to the car, waiting for Wyatt to peek out from under the hood. She wasn't going to make it to the store if she didn't leave within the next five minutes.

"That battery is as old as the damned car. I'm surprised it started even once. It's not charging properly."

"Can't you get it going just one more time? I have to take the berries to the store before it closes. I promised. Tom is waiting. If I don't get there, he might not take them."

"The old workhorse isn't going anywhere until you buy a new battery. The car ought to be checked out by a mechanic before you drive it again. Doesn't look like anything's been done to it in a long time."

She let out a grunt of exasperation. There was no time, not to mention money, for that. "Right now, the berries and my reliable reputation are at stake."

"Get in the truck. I'll drive you and the berries to town."

She watched him load the bushels into the pick-up, and then he grimaced and rotated his right shoulder before jumping into the cab.

She yanked off the old hat and used it as a fan. She must be a sight. Unexpectedly self-conscious by the nearness of Wyatt, a wave of desire shook her confidence. She scooted closer to the passenger door, smoothed her hair, pulled on her shorts, and put her berry-stained hands in her pockets. "Uh—thanks for helping me."

Without answering, he threw the transmission into reverse and backed the truck out of the driveway.

She released her ponytail holder and shook her head to let her hair fall down her back, took a deep breath, and closed her eyes. She was going to make it on time because of Wyatt.

He'd helped by fixing the bathroom and now she was in his debt again. After her divorce, she'd vowed to never again be obligated to another man. Was she making a mistake by getting Wyatt's help? Would he use her indebtedness to him against her?

**\*\*\***

The next day, impatience caused Amy to pace. She had to wait until Nan brought Bobby to the farm tomorrow. The moving van had already brought his furniture. Just as she'd thought, the navy plaid bedspread and curtains looked wonderful in the pale blue of the newly painted bedroom.

She unpacked his favorite toys and placed them in the toy box. Bobby's brown bear "Ted" sat on the bed waiting for him. He probably missed Ted, but he still had Billy the Duck with him. A smile pulled her lips as she remembered seeing her son under the covers asleep with Ted and Billy on either side of him.

She should feel good. The will was being probated and everything seemed to be going as planned. The apples were about to be picked and would be on their way to market. She had a little money in the bank and, as long as there was no unforeseen expense...

She crossed her fingers and didn't think about the old Volvo with its dead battery still sitting in the driveway. The car could be dealt with—later. She wouldn't let it dampen the joy she was feeling now.

The old screen door squeaked and she knew Wyatt had entered the kitchen. They were going to survey Granny's property, including the many acres she'd never seen. Even as a kid, she'd stayed around the old farmhouse and only occasionally wandered into the orchards to pick an apple. She hadn't realized how big the property was until Monday's meeting in the judge's office when she'd seen a map of the orchards and the surrounding land.

Wyatt seemed to know Granny's place well and had suggested they view it together.

She was surprised to see him drive the truck into the driveway pulling a horse trailer.

He jumped out of the cab and grinned at her. "I thought the best way to look at the place was by horseback. Granny told me you used to spend most of your summers riding."

"That's true. But I haven't ridden since I left home to go to college."

"It's like a bicycle. Once you know how you never forget. You used to vault, didn't you? Granny mentioned it."

"Yeah, when I was a kid."

"Then riding should be a breeze."

"Do you think it would be okay? It's been so long." She grinned at the thought of riding again, regardless of her concern that she'd make a fool of herself in front of him.

He backed one of the horses out of the trailer. "Don't worry. This old man is Sal, a gelding. One of the sweetest guys you'll ever meet. If you don't know what to do, just talk to him. He'll do what needs to be done. Won't you, old boy?" he cooed.

She was astounded by the gentleness he displayed toward the sorrel. And the horse seemed to respond to him.

"He's beautiful." She gently patted his blaze. "Is he yours?"

"Yeah, and so is this young man." The stallion snorted. "Now that the trailer door is open, he's impatient to get out. His name is "Spirit" for obvious reasons. Come on boy, I know you want to run."

The horse's black coat glistened in the sun. The smell of leather and steed filled her nostrils. Some might find the odor offensive. She got comfort from the happy memories of a childhood spent riding.

She held Sal's reins and mounted the wonderful charger. He stood and allowed her weight. "It's been so long. It's amazing to be on horseback again."

Wyatt sat astride Spirit as the horse pranced in place, their heads held high, their movements in harmony. *A magnificent pair.*

"Ready to go?" he asked.

61

# CHAPTER 7

**Wyatt** watched Amy. She was dressed in blue jeans, sneakers, and the same pink tank top she had worn when he first saw her at the bus stop. She flicked her fire-touched hair back and placed a huge pair of dark glasses on her small nose as her full lips pouted.

She looked good waiting to ride. She looked good with berry-stained hands, nails broken, and hair disheveled. She smiled at him. Damn, she just looked good, ripe, and ready.

"I thought we'd start in the north orchard and work our way around," he shouted.

"Okay."

It was clear by her expression that she was unaware of her sex appeal or how he was responding to it. She rode in silence. Yeah, she was sexy, but he had no intention of acting on his male inclinations. Still, he admired the rhythm of horse and rider.

She moved naturally, stayed fluid, didn't tighten up, and rocked with the animal instead of resisting the beast as many other women had when he'd invited them to ride.

Amy seemed fascinated with the panorama before her. Today would be a day of rediscovery for her. Time enough later for her to learn the weight of responsibility and accountability the land demanded from an owner. Soon, she'd understand that a sale of the property was the best thing for her.

A twinge in his back reminded him to move carefully. This was his first time back in the saddle since being thrown from a bucking bronco.

Spirit snorted. He wanted his head, needed to gallop in front of Sal as he always did. But Wyatt reined him in. *Sorry boy, maybe when we get to the meadow.* For now, they'd stay on the trail and take it easy.

The path widened and there was room for the two horses to ride side by side as they had done many times before, Spirit just slightly ahead of Sal.

"How did you get involved in the rodeo?" Amy broke the silence.

"Granny and your grandpa introduced me to it. They took me when I was a teenager. They could see I needed something to focus on besides my problems."

"I never knew. I mean I saw you around the farm, but I didn't think…"

"You were a little girl. I was a wild teen after my mom died. Granny kept you separated from me. I can smile now, but in those days, I was trouble. The rodeo was as untamed as I was and just what I needed."

He swiped his brow with the back of his hand and remembered. "The rodeo animals looked me in the eye and said, 'Your mom died and your dad doesn't want you near him. Hey, you think you've got it tough? You don't know from tough.' Then the horses would take turns throwing me on my ass and snorting in my face."

"And you got back on again?"

"I watched them buck to get a guy off their backs only to have another cowboy get in the saddle. They knocked him off too. Again, and again, they sent cowboys onto their backsides. But there was always another man ready to try. It taught me respect for the animals and I learned tenacity. By the time I could stay in the saddle for more than eight seconds, I was too damned worn out to be ornery, too exhausted to go out and cause trouble."

They both laughed.

"It's all thanks to your granddad and his love of horses."

"I never knew Grandpa cared about them that much. All I remember was him talking about apple trees."

"What I heard from the old timers around here was that he was a budding jockey when he was a kid. He just grew too tall for that dream to happen. But he never lost his love of horses."

"Well, I never…"

"If times had been different, he might have been a trainer. I know he wanted to start a breeding farm. There's an old corral out here."

"I'd love to see it."

"Okay."

The horses sauntered as Wyatt listened to the sounds of the foothills, the rustle of the leaves and the call of a crow. He glanced at Amy. She scanned the panorama too. The corners of her mouth turned up into a smile.

"I thought the trail would be all overgrown."
"Granny didn't mind, so I often brought horses here to exercise," Wyatt said. "It kept the trail open and I couldn't think of a more beautiful place to ride. The

sky's blue and the air is clean. In some of the cities where I travel, the air's become so polluted a person would be better off inside. Nice for the animals to breathe good air here on the farm."

"San Francisco has pretty good air. But one of the things that got to me was the twenty-four-seven noise, sirens, and car horns. It's quiet here. Peaceful. I can hear myself think."

He watched as she pushed her sunglasses up on the bridge of her nose and viewed an eagle soar and then circle in the clear sky.

"I love it here. I hope Bobby does too."

"Any kid would."

"When I was little, I'm afraid I didn't. I thought it was boring. I spent my childhood thinking about living in the city. Telling Granny that's where I was going to live when I grew up. I wish I could tell her how much the farm means to me now." She sniffed. "I had this crazy idea that living in the city with the fancy stores and high-rise buildings would be paradise." She shook her head. "Stupid."

"I guess that's the grass is always greener syndrome."

"I'd love to let her know how wrong I was."

They rode past the last row of apple trees and toward a stand of Ponderosas. Pine needles and cones littered the area. Shaded by the trees, the air was somewhat cooler and the breeze became saturated with the scent of pine.

"There's a lot of timber up here. Your Grandpa talked about clearing some of it and increasing the apple output. He had a lot of ideas, but like many people, lack of funds got in the way of his big plans."

"I know he talked about planting some of the "newfangled" apples, as he called them. There are so many new types now." She adjusted her position in the saddle and pushed her hair out of her face. "The Red Delicious has lots of competition these days. Guess he hoped to plant new orchards of Spartans or Galas or..."

They let the horses gallop, then slowed them to a canter before stopping in a meadow for a moment, and then continued up the trail.

"The Christmas trees are up ahead." Wyatt pointed.

"As a kid, it was one of my proudest moments when Grandpa let me choose a tree for the town holiday display."

She reined in the horse. "The trees are so big now."

She looked like a little kid on Christmas morning. He smiled. "You've got a good crop. The last few years your grandmother was too sick to cut and sell them, so they just kept growing. She told me the apples and the berries were all she could manage."

Her smile vanished. "I didn't know. I should have understood. Should have asked Granny, but I didn't. I'm not making excuses, but she wasn't the kind of woman to ask for help."

"No." He watched the joy drain from Amy's features. He should have just let her enjoy the place. Now a frown marred her pretty face.

They rode in silence.

A granite outcropping narrowed the trail and they slowed the horses. "Hold up, boy." He waited for Amy to join him.

"I used to crawl all over these rocks as a kid, but I never noticed how stunningly beautiful they are."

"Funny how kids love climbing on things. Too bad city kids only have the fake rock walls in the gym to climb on."

"I think I'll pass on climbing them today." She laughed.

"Probably a good idea."

His stallion pawed the ground and snorted. "Listen, why don't you stay here for a couple of minutes? There's an open meadow ahead. I'm going to let Spirit have a little exercise. I'll be right back."

"Okay."

He let Spirit have his head and felt the horse spring into action under him. The stallion wasn't the only one who needed the exercise. Being around Amy made his blood pulse and his body heat.

***

Wyatt and the animal were breathing hard when he reined the stallion to a walk and turned back. *Amy's waiting.*

She grinned when she saw him. "You two make a great team."

He shrugged. "The old corral is down there behind the grove of trees. When we get there, we'll take a break."

"Great."

The remnants of a fence poked through the tall golden grass. But the corral was basically a ruin. He tied up the horses to a Manzanita bush. Then he helped Amy off the tall mount, holding her to him, feeling her softness and breathing in her floral perfume, before setting her on the ground.

"Thanks." She rubbed her backside. "Wow, it's been too long since I've been in the saddle. No muscle memory." She chuckled.

"There's some shade over here." He glanced at her nicely shaped rear and then took a bed roll from Spirit's western saddle and tucked it under his arm. He walked toward a huge spreading oak.

He slowed his stride as she rushed to keep up with him. They passed through the meadow to the small stand of California black oaks. With the blanket rolled out under one of the trees, he sat down. He pulled out two bottles of water from a pocket in the blanket. He handed one of them to Amy.

She drank the water and then sank slowly onto the blanket next to him. "I think I'm going to be sore tomorrow. But it's worth it. I love riding." She pushed her sunglasses to the top of her head. "I like the farmland best in the spring. As a kid, I remember the rolling hills in bloom with wildflowers. Blue lupines covered this meadow. They're my favorite flower." Her eyes sparkled with excitement. "The word means Wolf in Latin."

He stared at her.

"Weird, I know. When I was a kid, I spent a lot of time looking things up in the library."

"You were a bookworm. And you wore horn-rim glasses. I remember you."

"Yeah. Thank goodness for contact lenses."

He laughed, hugged her then quickly let her go. "I shouldn't have done that."

"I'm glad you did."

Her response startled him. What would she say if he kissed her? Was he crazy to even think of it?

He reached for her. She came willingly and pressed close to him. The smell of vanilla from her shampoo wafted to him and he felt the warmth of her small breasts as they pressed against his chest. He gazed down at her. Her eyelids fluttered closed and her lips parted.

His lips brushed hers. Then, with a sigh, he took her mouth. It softened under his. He deepened the kiss with the penetration of his tongue. A small moan escaped her. Her breathing quickened. He pulled away when his breathing increased too.

*What the hell am I doing?* This wasn't part of his plan. It was against his better judgment to kiss her and damn, he wanted to do it again.

She adjusted her tank top, jumped up from the blanket and ran out to a patch of blue lupines. While he admired her, he saw her pretend to admire an exceptionally well-formed flower. She picked it as he caught up with her. "The last one of summer." She held it up to him. "Autumn is almost here," she said lightly.

"It's getting late. We better get back."

They didn't talk on the way back to the barn.

When they got to the farmhouse, he helped her down and she ran inside. He heard the kitchen door close behind her.

The horses needed him. He went straight to the barn to cool them down. Then he'd pump iron to cool himself down.

***

Amy leaned against the back door and listened to her pounding heart. *Calm down.* With her hand to her chest, she tried to stop the hammering.

69

This day had turned out to be much more emotional than she could have ever imagined. She anticipated being affected by seeing the land. She didn't think Wyatt would kiss her or that she'd respond to his kiss with so much need.

The hot air of the kitchen surrounded her. Fresh air was what she needed, but she didn't want to run into Wyatt again. She threw open the window and inhaled. Seeing him would be more than she could handle right now.

No matter how much her body reacted to his touch, men were persona non grata in her life. After the divorce from Robert almost four years ago, she'd realized she didn't need them. All she wanted was to raise Bobby alone. no men, no sex, no problem. She was fine with that.

Without knowing what he was doing to her, Wyatt had touched a nerve with his kiss. Longing for him pulsed through her. Desire threatened to overwhelm her. That wouldn't do either of them any good. Wyatt had changed everything for her, but he didn't need to understand it.

Sophie had told her about Wyatt's women. Young beauties followed him on the rodeo circuit, groupies much more gorgeous than Amy could ever manage. They had volunteered to be his, whenever he wanted to take them.

For him, the kiss was just a nice time spent on a warm summer outing, nothing more. He'd probably gone on many such outings with better outcomes.

"You mean nothing to him," she whispered trying to brand the idea on her brain. *Nothing.*

"Enough!" *You're being ridiculous, acting like a teenager. You're a grown woman with a child.*

Okay, it didn't matter that since the first day she'd seen him so many years ago in high school, she'd wondered what it would be like to kiss him. Today's kiss made her body sing and it was far better than any she'd imagined in her daydreams. His skin was hot, muscles taut, mouth soft, whoa, definitely better than her imagination. But that was no reason to run from him as if she were a scared kid running from her first kiss.

Shoulders back, hand on the doorknob, she opened the kitchen door and walked toward the barn. The least she could do was behave like a grownup and help with the horses.

The barn smelled of new oats when she entered. The horses were in their stalls, saddles and tack already removed. The horses didn't even bother to whiny when she came near.

The lights over the exercise equipment were on. As she moved closer, she could hear grunts coming from the area. Wyatt was on his back on the weight bench pressing an enormous weight above him. He set the weight on the stand and sat up.

Dressed in only jeans, the deep breath he took expanded his muscled chest, and his golden torso glistened with moisture. When she saw her, one eyebrow rose as if to ask, what are you doing here? Or, I certainly didn't expect to see you here. She wasn't sure which.

"I came to help with the horses."

"Done." He grabbed a big towel from a hook near the bench and wiped his abs."

She couldn't stop staring as he made small circles on his skin.

His mouth turned up slightly at the corners and she was barely aware that he had moved a few steps closer. "I'll give them some feed when they're completely cooled down."

Before she realized what he was doing, he'd thrown the towel around her as a lasso and held her. He pulled her to him and his mouth came down to meet hers.

Her lips parted to speak, but it was too late. His tongue teased hers. Without her volition, her tongue teased back. She couldn't pull away from what he offered because she wanted it more than he did.

As her lips opened further, she reached forward and pulled him nearer to her. He pressed against her until their hips met. She sighed and ran her hand through his thick hair. Her eyes closed as she tasted him.

He walked her back a couple of steps, still holding her to him, and slowly, gently, lowered her to the fresh hay by the stall. The smell of man, hay, and leather sent a shot of adrenaline through her body and her hips jerked upward.

His tongue fluttered around the nape of her neck and her body tingled. She moaned and he returned to kiss her again.

Tenderly, he caressed her breasts. *Too long.* It had been so long since she'd been touched. She didn't know her body would cry out for it. But it wasn't a response she would have from any man. Only Wyatt's embrace could cause her thunderous reactions.

Her heart slammed against her rib cage when he slid the strap of her tank top off her shoulder. Her breathing quickened. His breath was rapid too. Soon their inhalations became synchronized.

"Mommy. Mommy."

Amy pulled away from Wyatt and jerked to a sitting position. "It's my son, Bobby. I have to go to him."

# CHAPTER 8

"**I** thought Bobby wasn't coming here until tomorrow," Wyatt said, brushing hay from his jeans.

"Me too," Amy whispered.

"Amy, where are you?"

"That's Nan. She's taking care of Bobby." Amy jumped up. "I'll be right there," she shouted and hoped her friend would stay outside. She ran from the barn and the door slammed behind her.

Nan, dressed in black jeans, a black t-shirt, and a hooded sweatshirt, her hand on her slim hip, stared at her.

"God girl, at least fix your bra and get the straw out of your hair before Bobby sees you," she scolded.

"Where is he?"

"I told him to get back in the car and wait until I found you. If you like, I can take him to a fast-food place so you can finish what you've started."

"Don't be ridiculous, it's not like that. I've been waiting for days to see Bobby. Anyway, there's no "fast food" in town."

Wyatt came out of the barn. Still shirtless, he nodded as he walked by Nan, but he didn't stop.

"Is *that* the handyman?" Nan whispered.

"Hush, he can hear you. He's not a handyman. Well, I mean he is— sort of. Uh, it's a long story."

"I just bet *he* is. And it looks like you were ready to take all of it." Nan winked, unzipped the hooded shirt, and fluffed her short spiky brown hair. "It's hot up here."

"Nan, for pity's sake." Amy saw her friend's mouth open wide about to speak again. "I'm warning you." She glared at her friend but couldn't help smiling. The woman always spoke her mind and called things like she saw them. That was one of the reasons they got along. She always knew where she stood with Nan.

She watched her friend stare at Wyatt until he disappeared into the cottage.

"Girlfriend, I didn't think you had it in you. I leave you on your own for a short time and you do all right. More than all right." She reached up and yanked a piece of straw from Amy's hair and laughed. "Does he have a brother?"

Amy rolled her eyes and yanked the strap of her top up before she walked toward her friend's car parked at the end of the driveway.

"Mommy!" Bobby ran from the car and jumped into her arms.

"Honey, I missed you so much." She kissed his cheek and ruffled his strawberry-blonde hair. His blue eyes sparkled. Always small for his age, he seemed smaller, paler. Maybe it was because she'd grown stronger and tanner since coming to the hot climate, while her son had been living in the foggy city.

"Can we get a doggie now?"

Amy laughed and hugged him again. "I missed you baby."

"But can we?"

Wyatt appeared in the doorway of the barn. Amy hadn't seen him return from the cottage.

Bobby wiggled out of her arms. "Mommy, who's that?"

"Uh." She glanced at Wyatt.

He grinned but didn't say anything.

"Mommy?"

"He takes care of the horses."

"We have horses?" Bobby ran into the barn before she could stop him.

They ran after Bobby. Wyatt got there first with Amy and Nan close behind.

"Be careful. Don't get too close," Amy shouted.

Bobby stopped and stared at the first horse. "He's big."

"Yes, *he* is." Nan elbowed Amy and looked sideways at Wyatt.

"Nan, I'm going to kill you," she whispered.

"Mister, can I ride the horsy?"

Wyatt smiled. "Maybe tomorrow, if it's okay with your mother, but now, the horses have to go to bed." He winked at Amy.

Her cheeks flushed. Surprised by his kindness, she couldn't help grinning too. Why had Sophie said Wyatt didn't like kids?

Did he like them or was he only trying to, as her Granny used to say, "Get into her panties?"

She watched Wyatt go to the weight bench, grab his shirt, and pull it on.

She cleared her throat. "Baby, come into the house and I'll show you your room. It has new paint and…"

"I want to touch the horsy."

"I don't know…"

Amy looked up and found Wyatt standing next to her. Without a word, he picked up Bobby and held him. "The horse likes to be touched, but there are a couple of rules first."

"Okay." Bobby put his arm around Wyatt's neck.

"First rule, never yell and wave your hands around the animal. He might get scared and never stand behind him. He could kick you by accident."

Bobby's eyes widened.

"It's okay. The horsy won't hurt you. This is Sal. He's a nice old boy. He likes you to rub right here just above his nose." Wyatt demonstrated.

The little boy slowly reached out and softly rubbed the horse. He giggled and patted him again.

"Okay, Bobby, that's enough for now." She reached for him.

Wyatt set him down and he ran to her. "His hair is soft Mommy. Do you want to touch him?"

Amy watched Wyatt. "Maybe tomorrow." Her cheeks flushed again.

"Thank you." She hesitated. "Do you want to join us in the house for dinner?"

"Got plans."

"Oh." For the first time in recent memory, jealousy crawled up her spine. *Of course, he has dinner plans with another woman.*

"See you tomorrow, big guy."

"Night, mister."

"Bobby, this is Mr. Cameron."

"Call me Wyatt."

"Okay."

"See you, Amy."

"Yeah." She felt Wyatt scan her.

"Mommy, why is your face red?"

Wyatt walked out of the barn and the door slammed closed.

"It's nothing, Bobby. Too much sun I guess." Her voice didn't sound like her own, too high. She cleared her throat. "Nan, you're staying the night?"

"Can't. I have to work tomorrow. If I leave now, I'll be back in the city by eleven o'clock. I got the food you wanted for Bobby and ten pounds of gluten-free flour and some organic brown rice."

"That's great. I can't thank you enough. Thank goodness there is more gluten-free food in the stores these days. Even so, I haven't had a chance to check in Sierra Creek yet. Nan, stay long enough to have some food."

"Can't. Just invite me back and find out Wyatt has a brother."

They both laughed and Amy hugged her BFF. "Drive carefully."

"Yeah, yeah." Nan hugged Bobby. "See you."

Together, she and Bobby watched Nan get in the small car and drive away. Her son waved with one arm while he wrapped the other one around her leg.

"Come on, time to get ready for bed." She took hold of his small hand, walked into the farmhouse, and shut the door. "Bobby, this is your new home."

***

Bobby sat at the breakfast table eating oatmeal. Amy took a seat next to him and sipped coffee.

"Do doggies and horses like to play together?" he asked, his mouth full of cereal.

She stifled a laugh. "Swallow before you talk."

He gulped and said, "Do they?"

"I don't know, but the horses are just visiting. They belong to Wyatt and he's only staying in the cottage for a little while."

Bobby frowned and pushed his bowl away. His bottom lip stuck out. His brow knitted further. Without warning, he jumped up and ran out of the room.

"Where are you going?"

She ran after him.

He was yanking on the barn door by the time she reached him.

Wyatt opened it and let him in. "Ready for your ride, big guy?"

"Do doggies and horses like to play together?"

Not missing a beat, Wyatt answered, "Sometimes." He smiled.

"Cause my mommy said I could get a dog. But I want a horse too."

"I said maybe we could get a dog. We'll have to check it out."

"Come on Bobby, let's see about going for a ride."

Amy sucked in a big breath of air. Wyatt was really going to put her baby on the back of a horse. Until this moment, she hadn't considered just what that meant. Sal was huge. She'd practically grown up on a horse. But she worried because Bobby was small for his age and delicate. It'd be easy for him to slip out of Sal's saddle and fall.

# CHAPTER 9

**"You** and your mom wait. I'll bring Sal out."

When the sorrel quarter horse left the barn, he looked bigger than he had yesterday when Amy rode him.

"Don't worry," Wyatt said. "I'll take it easy. You'll be fine, won't you, big guy?"

"Can I ride now?" Bobby said showing no fear.

He took the boy's hand and lifted him onto Sal's back. "Just sit there for a minute. See this?" He pointed to the saddle horn. "You can hold on to that. It's okay. Hold on. I'll make sure you don't fall."

The little boy grabbed the horn with both hands and grinned.

"Now these are the reins. They tell the horse which way you want him to go. Right or left."

Amy watched her son, a serious expression on his boyish face. His tiny hands holding onto the saddle horn for dear life, his knuckles white. She yanked her smartphone out of her pocket and took a photo of him. And hoping Wyatt wouldn't notice, she took one of him too and then another when he wasn't looking at her.

"We're going to walk Sal around the yard. We tell him to move by saying giddy up."

"Giddy up." Bobby giggled.

Sal moved forward and strolled the length of the yard. Wyatt was beside him, his hand supporting Bobby's back as they went.

"Mommy, look at me." Her son ginned. "Giddy up."

Wyatt let the horse move a little faster and jogged alongside.

"Look, Mommy. Look."

"I see. Hold on tight." She snapped another photo.

Wyatt jogged for a little longer and then said, "Easy boy." The horse slowed and then stopped and he picked Bobby off the horse and held him. "You did great. You're a natural."

"What does that mean?"

"Means you did a good job." Wyatt smiled.

"I did good, Mommy." Bobby ran to her.

"Yes, you did and I have photos to prove it." She hugged him and showed him the pictures on her phone, skipping the ones she'd taken of Wyatt.

"I'm thirsty."

"Go and get a drink, but drink slowly."

Bobby ran toward the house.

"I'll be right there," she shouted. "Thanks, Wyatt. You're good with kids."

He shrugged.

"He'll never forget it."

"I meant what I said. He's a natural. Most kids freeze up the first time they get on a horse, especially someone his age. It seems a long way down to the ground when you're that small."

"It scared me just to watch him, but I could see he was having fun."

"He should have lessons."

81

"Maybe someday, I can't afford them now. Come into the house for a cool drink."

"I'm taking Sal out for a workout, then going into town. You can catch a ride with me if you want."

"Thanks. I'd like that. I need to pick up a couple of things at the health food store."

***

It was almost one pm when Amy leaned back in the Ford and watched Wyatt slowly maneuver the truck down Sierra Creek's crowded main street.

"I don't think I've ever seen it so busy." She gazed out the passenger side window. "I thought there'd be fewer people since the mill closed two years ago."

"A lot of the old timers come to town on Saturday to do their shopping for the week or even for the month."

She watched as people scurried on the raised sidewalks into and out of the stores.

"Mommy, look a horse." Bobby pointed to a buckskin tied to the hitching post out in front of the general store.

"I don't see a parking space anywhere. I should have ridden a horse." Wyatt joked.

"I guess the tourists are still in town."

"Yeah, plenty of them looking for gold in the Mokelumne River or going to see the old tailing wheels, and then buy some rock candy in town."

"What's rock candy?" Bobby asked.

"Candy made of sugar, but it looks like rock crystals, quarts, amethyst, and such," Wyatt said.

"Can we get some, Mommy?"

"We'll see."

"Sophie sells it at her store." Wyatt pointed to the ice cream parlor as the truck continued down the street at a snail's pace.

"If I could get even half of the visitors to come to Granny's farm and spend just one dollar, the farm would be self-supporting," Amy said almost to herself.

"Sierra Creek's a perfect place for a day trip from Sacramento. They just need a reason to drive to the farm," Wyatt agreed.

Amy rubbed her forehead and tried to think of one.

"Hi, Wyatt." A young woman with blonde hair and big brown eyes yelled and waved. "Wyatt!"

"Cowboy, you're back in town," a brunette shouted from an open doorway.

He glanced at the woman, but didn't answer. Instead, he kept driving.

"I'm waiting for you to phone me." A shapely teen grinned at Wyatt, then glared at Amy.

"You're a celebrity. Sophie told me, but I had no idea."

Another woman waved but had the good sense not to yell at him.

"It's embarrassing." He took a quick look at Amy. "I shouldn't have gone on that damned TV talk show. Ever since then, they've been driving me crazy."

"Oh." She laughed and he joined her.

A sedan with Nevada license plates pulled out of a parking space and he parked the truck. "I'm going to The Hitching Post to pick up some new tack. It shouldn't take long. Why don't we meet at Sophie's Ice cream parlor? I'll buy you and Bobby a sundae and Bobby can pick out some rock candy."

"Can we?" Bobby pulled on her sleeve.

"Okay." She jumped out of the truck and helped Bobby down.

"Wyatt, can I have chocolate ice cream?"

"It's up to your mommy. If she says—"

"Sugar!"

A woman rushed up to Wyatt and grabbed him in a bear hug. Surprised, Amy watched the woman plant a kiss on his open mouth and then wipe her red lipstick off his lips.

"Sugar, why didn't you tell me you were coming to town?"

Tall, with long black hair, blue eyes and white teeth surrounded by full lips painted red, the woman grinned. Black denim stuck tight to her ass and a red spandex top squeezed her chest to display her voluminous breasts. She gracefully stood on her tippy-toes in four-inch stilettos and planted another kiss squarely on Wyatt's tightened mouth, then threaded her arm with his as if she meant to walk away with him.

"I just adored the ravioli dinner we shared the other night. It was scrumptious." She wiggled her rear end and then blew him a kiss. "I should watch my figure, but who could resist you and ravioli?" She licked her lips.

He froze in place, his hands at his side. An expression of a man whose shirt collar had suddenly tightened to choke him spread across his face.

So, Wyatt's modus operandi was to bring Italian dinner to his women. Amy had been stupid enough to think he'd bought it only for her.

"I guess he isn't going to introduce us. I'm Charlene." The woman interrupted Amy's thoughts.

"Amy," she said in a weak voice.

Charlene stared at her. "I know you. You used to live with that funny old "Apple lady" out on Star Route Three."

With a frown, Amy hid her berry-stained hands behind her back and closed her lips tight, not daring to talk or she'd say something to Charlene that she'd regret later.

She scanned the woman, five foot eleven if not six feet tall, freckle free, olive skin, and straight smooth hair.

At five feet three inches tall, Amy had never considered her height or her bust size one way or the other. But now, she appreciated she was short, flat, not to mention pale and badly dressed in old jeans and a big t-shirt.

She squinted through her thick glasses. *Damn.* She should have taken the time to change her clothes and put in her contact lenses. Not that it would have made much difference. She'd still be short and have a flat chest. But at least she couldn't be thought of as "four eyes," her high school nickname.

Charlene continued a steady stream of talk at Wyatt, but Amy had lost track of the conversation.

"And who's this adorable little man?"

Amy bristled when the flirt turned her charms on the only other man in the area—Bobby.

Her son's eyes widened as he stared at the woman and a sloppy smile spread across his face. "I'm Bobby." He grinned.

Even her son was charmed by the flashy woman. *Traitor.*

"Well, aren't you just the cutest thing?" Charlene's white teeth blazed.

Unconsciously, Amy pulled Bobby closer, holding him by his shoulders with both hands.

"Is he your son?" she asked.

"Yeah."

"And where's his daddy?"

"He lives in San Francisco."

"Well, you won't mind if I take Wyatt away for a little while. Will you?"

Surprised by the change of subject, she pushed her glasses up on the bridge of her nose and before she could answer, she watched the woman pull on Wyatt's arm until he walked with her.

"Come on Bobby, we'll go to the health food store. Afterward, I'll buy you a sherbet."

"Wyatt's going to buy me chocolate."

"He's busy. We'll get our stuff and then I'll borrow Sophie's car and take you home."

"But Mommy…"

"Come on."

The joy of seeing Bobby eat his raspberry sherbet was tempered by the fact that Wyatt wasn't there as he promised.

***

At ten pm that evening, Amy heard Wyatt's truck pull into the driveway. Bobby was asleep and she hoped the truck's engine didn't wake him.

In her bathrobe, she didn't look out of the kitchen window to the cottage. Instead, was about to leave the room when she heard a knock at the backdoor.

"Open the door. Amy, I know you're up," Wyatt said as he banged on the door. "I have something for Bobby." Anger deepened his voice.

She tightened the belt of her cotton bathrobe and reached for the door handle. Should she open it? Before she could decide, he pushed the door open and entered the room. His eyes sparked as he scanned her. She stepped back from him.

"Darn it, Amy, I thought you were going to wait for me today."

"I know what men are like when they're—busy." Without realizing it, she rubbed her arm where Robert had often left bruises when he grabbed her and hit her for interrupting him.

"I'm not Robert."

She startled. "What do you know about my ex-husband?"

"Granny told me."

"What?"

"Let's just say, I'd never do anything to hurt you."

She blinked. How many times had Roberts promised he'd never hit her again?

"You don't have to worry about me or my moods. I don't hit women." He hesitated. "Even so, you're extremely annoying. I went to Sophie's to meet you. You weren't there. She told me you took her car and went home." He ran his hands over the back of his neck. "Never mind, I bought some rock candy for Bobby." He set the bag of candy on the table.

"Thank you." She clutched the bag to her. "He'll be pleased."

"I've tried to keep my promise to Granny to help you and I'll continue to do it. But I don't owe you information about my social life. It's none of your business. And that's the most explaining I've ever done. Don't expect me to ever do it again."

The door banged closed behind him. The shock of the slamming door reverberated in the quiet room. Stunned, she stood staring, frozen in place.

*What should I do now?*

# CHAPTER 10

**Amy** sat at Granny's Limbert desk in the downstairs den and glanced at the calendar. Hard to believe a week had gone by since Wyatt brought the rock candy for Bobby.

Since then, she'd made sure she and Wyatt were never alone. He worked on the farm fixing what he'd apparently promised he'd do for Granny.

Today once again, he'd mentioned the fixes he'd make that would help when she put the farm on the market, something she didn't plan to do.

Maybe it was her perverse personality, but the more often he said to sell, the more determined she was to stay and make the farm pay.

Bobby and Wyatt had slipped into the habit of a morning ride while she made breakfast for them. If anyone had looked in on them, they'd appear to be an all-American family, mom, dad, and son.

Earlier, Bobby had gobbled down his egg white omelet and then run out to see Wyatt. She hoped her son wasn't getting to close to him. Was he beginning to think of him as a dad? Wyatt was nothing more than a temporary acquaintance at best and at worst. She wouldn't go there.

Still, she'd kept her silence because she hadn't seen Bobby warm to any man since Robert had hit him. Around other guys, he was silent and clung very close to her side. With Wyatt, Bobby was a carefree kid with an easy grin.

She glanced out of the window. Both Bobby and Wyatt were laughing. He put his arm around her son's shoulder as if they were buddies.

If she were honest with herself, she'd admit she wanted Wyatt. His kind demeanor and physical attributes made her wonder what he'd be like when his passion was aroused. With his hunger unleashed, could she handle his touch deep within her core? She yanked her gaze away from him.

*Regardless of how he treats your son, he wants to sell this place and that makes Wyatt an adversary. He's ready to take away Bobby's birthright.*

She took a deep breath to push down her anger and returned her attention to the website she'd put up to advertise Granny's Organic Apples. It was an attempt to entice tourists to visit the farm. A few tourist dollars could go a long way to help make the place self-supporting.

There was still a lot to do before she could welcome anyone. She opened a folder of digital photos she'd taken of the farm. Decisions about which ones she wanted to upload to the site had to be made. And she'd found Granny's Apple recipes. Should she put those up as well?

"Wyatt, can I paint?" Her son shouted in excitement.

She gazed out the den window again. Wyatt was just taking Bobby's hand. He looked so fragile next to the cowboy.

"I have a special job for you, big guy. I'm going to paint the cottage. It's going to need a sign. I want you to paint the wood for it."

"Me?"

"Yup. I put the sign on the drop cloth over there on the lawn. I'll carry the paint and you bring the brush. You can do it while I work on the cottage."

"Okay," Bobby agreed.

Her heart warmed as she watched him copy the way Wyatt had dipped the little brush into a small can of paint. At four and a half years old, she wouldn't have let him use real paint. Even so, Wyatt had given him the white paint and brush and set a task for him. Then he'd turned from her son to work on the cottage. To his favor, he kept twisting to glance back at Bobby.

The two of them were covered in paint when they came to the kitchen for lunch.

"Mommy, look at my sign."

Wyatt carried the board to the back door. "We better leave it out here until it's completely dry."

"Do you see it? Wyatt helped me print the word."

*"Cottage"* was written in black letters over the white background. "It's wonderful." She hugged him without realizing his clothes had wet paint on them.

"Mommy, now you have paint on you too." He laughed.

"And I didn't even have to do the work." She giggled. "Come on you two, time for lunch. Wash your hands."

***

Wyatt finished eating, excused himself, and left as soon as he could without being rude. The sign that Bobby painted was still sitting on the back porch. He picked it up and took it to the cottage and nailed it to a post on the front porch.

The little boy was standing at the back door watching. He gave the boy a thumbs-up. The kid returned the signal.

"Good job, kid."

"It's almost time to go. You have to change your clothes for preschool." Wyatt heard Amy shout.

He looked back at the house. Bobby was gone from the doorway. With his strawberry blonde hair, blue eyes and a big grin, the little guy was getting to him. That surprised him. Until he'd met Amy's son, he'd thought of kids as rug rats.

He'd noticed Bobby's lips tightened when he first sat on the horse, eyes wide and his knuckles white as he clutched the saddle horn. But he didn't cry, didn't ask for his mommy. The next day he'd asked to ride again.

It never occurred to him a child could have so much personality. Small for his age and with a delicate build, he nonetheless had a heart of a lion and was eager for life's challenges.

Amy had appeared much less excited about him getting on a horse. Fear had shown in her eyes. Even so, she let him mount. She'd chewed on her bottom lip and held her hands to her heart, but when Bobby laughed and called to her, she'd waved and smiled.

He guessed she wanted to make sure her boy had a good experience, regardless of her concerns. The kid probably hadn't noticed, but her smile hadn't reached her eyes. Since then, Wyatt had admired how much she cared for her son and unlike his mother, even put Bobby's desires before her own.

His thoughts were cut short when Amy walked by the open back door. The scent of her vanilla shampoo and the sway of her sexy hips triggered a tightening of his body.

For the first time, he wondered what it'd be like to have a wife and kid of his own. What was he thinking? He looked away. Better get back to the rodeo circuit soon, before she got so far under his skin and he couldn't get her out of his system. Before she depended on him and even worse, he began to depend on her. Before he became so fond of them both, he couldn't leave.

**\*\*\***

Amy glanced out the living room window of the old farmhouse. She'd been putting off working in the front yard because her first concern had been for the fruit trees. The plan to open the farm to tourists where they could learn about farming, pick their own apples and buy organic pies and apple sauce was getting closer. The homestead had to look presentable, appealing, and be the quintessential organic farm and farmhouse. She wished there was a budget for a professional gardener to whip up a design for the yard, but there wasn't. It was her job.

With a deep breath, she went to Bobby's room.

"Come on, we're going out to the front yard to work. Why don't you take your truck? You can play while I mow the lawn and do some weeding. I'll let you plant some of the pretty flowers."

"Okay. Mommy, can we have a dog? A puppy could play with me when you work in the yard."

"Soon, you'll be so big you can mow the lawn."

"Oh, Mommy, when *can* I have a dog?"

"We'll see. Come on."

In the front yard, she adjusted her San Francisco Giants cap to shade her eyes and started to weed. "I promise I'll look into getting a dog—before long. But first, we'll have to choose what kind of a puppy we want."

Bobby grinned and ran off to play with his firetruck on a rock outcropping in the front yard.

"It's hotter than I thought, must be nearly a hundred degrees. Maybe you should sit on the porch for a bit to cool down. I don't want you to get overheated," she shouted.

He was busy making siren sounds for his truck.

"Did you hear me, Bobby? Don't get overheated."

"Where's Wyatt?"

"He went to the lumber yard. He'll be back in a bit."

She watched her son play and was grateful he finally had a yard where he was safe.

Most of the weeds came easily from the small bed in front of the living room window. Granny's old shovel leaned against the wall of the house, ready to be used if any were too big to be pulled out.

The old mower was dull and cutting the grass was tougher than she thought it would be. But she was getting in shape. When she first arrived at the farm it would have been impossible to finish without stopping to take a rest. Now she managed it without even becoming short of breath.

She heard Wyatt's truck before she saw it. She'd just finished working on the lawn when he drove into the driveway and turned off the engine.

"Looking good." He nodded at the grass and then glanced at her. His gaze traveled to her shorts and then to her bare legs.

"Thanks." She tugged on the back of her pants and made a mental note to get a pair of Bermuda shorts.

He jumped out of the cab and checked the load in the pick-up's bed. "I think I have enough lumber to take care of mending the corral."

"That's wonderful."

"Mommy, help!"

Amy ran to Bobby and grabbed him in her arms. A rattlesnake struck her before she saw it. She screamed and ran toward the house.

"Amy, stop!"

She continued to run, wanting to get Bobby out of danger.

"Now!" Wyatt shouted. "Sit down."

Still holding Bobby, she halted. "It was a snake."

"Did it bite you?"

"It rattled and then struck, but I think it missed me."

She pointed to the snake still coiled on the ground. Bobby trembled in her arms and she covered his eyes so he couldn't see the snake.

Wyatt grabbed the shovel leaning against the house and cut off the snake's head and then ran to her. "Sit down and let Bobby see the dead snake," he demanded. "The boy needs to know what a dangerous snake looks like."

"Big guy, see the diamond pattern on its back. Never touch a snake with that pattern, they're poisonous—uh—they have poison in their bite. But they usually rattle their warning before they strike, so you can get out of their way."

Bobby's eyes widened and he clutched Amy around her neck.

"Hey buddy, do you think you'd know it if you saw one again?"

"Yeah." Bobby nodded.

"Good boy." He used the shovel to toss the snake away from them. "Amy, let me take a look to make sure you weren't bitten."

"I think it just hit my shoe," she said hopefully. Her legs as well as her voice shook.

"If it got your shoe, don't touch it. The fangs and venom could be there. Let me check first." He knelt next to her and scanned her leg and then her ankle and her shoe. "Looks like the rattler nicked you."

She gasped when she saw the two fang marks near her ankle.

He ran to the truck and she watched as he took something from under the seat of the cab.

In the heat of the day, she shivered, and goose bumps popped out on her arms. As a child, she'd heard old timers tell of people who'd died from this kind of snake bite. People who, after being bitten, had run sending the venom coursing quickly through their system to the heart. She knew the stories and yet she had run too. What would have happened if Wyatt hadn't been there to tell her to stop?

He returned with a First Aid box and carefully slipped off her shoe and sock. "To be on the safe side, I have to make a cut and take out the poison with this suction kit. Breathe slowly and try to stay calm and keep your legs down lower than your heart. Ready?"

# CHAPTER 11

*Don't panic.* Amy tried to control her breathing and turned away from Wyatt.

"Bobby, I'm not going to hurt your mom, but I have to make a tiny cut to get the snake's poison out. I have this little suction cup. It will take the poison away." Wyatt held up the small rubber tube-like device. "See, son?"

She watched Bobby's eyes widen, but he didn't speak.

"Amy, here it goes."

She squeezed her eyes closed, bit her bottom lip and nodded. The cut was smooth and it wasn't until he made the opening bleed that the pain hit her. "Whoa. Stop. Quit." She tried to slap his hands away.

With one huge hand, he held hers tightly together. "Can't stop. Not yet. Have to get all the poison out. Stay calm. Slow breaths."

She held back sobs and took a deep breath. She had to be strong for Bobby's sake. But she was trembling and tears ran down her face. She hated being weak in front of him.

"Mommy, don't cry," her son whimpered.

"She's okay," Wyatt said his voice clear and strong. "Stay calm, Amy. Slow breathing. Yeah, that's good."

She watched him rip open a package of gauze. "Hold that in place while I cut a piece of tape. He lifted the gauze and bandaged the wound. She didn't see his Swiss Army knife until he wiped it on his jeans and stuck it back in his pocket.

"Come on Bobby. Let's get your mother to the hospital so the doctor can take a look at her."

Bobby's face flushed.

"Don't worry, she's going to be fine." Wyatt's arms flexed as he picked her up keeping her leg lower than her heart. She held on to him, thankful for his support. He set her on the passenger side of the truck and helped Bobby into the extended cab and buckled the boy's seat belt.

"You sure I need to go to the hospital? I feel okay." Her leg hurt like the devil.

"I think the poison's out, but let's play it safe and get some anti-venom and see if there's anything else you need."

She buckled her belt. She'd go to the hospital for Bobby's sake. He needed a healthy mom. Still, with no insurance, she didn't know how the heck she was going to pay for the emergency room visit.

***

Wyatt paced in the small bland waiting room of Sierra Creek County Medical Center. The acid in his stomach churned. Bobby was asleep on a nearby orange vinyl couch. Sleep, no doubt, was the boy's way of coping with a stressful situation.

The whole incident with the snake had taken less than twenty minutes from the bite to entering the hospital. Yet, Amy might have died in those few minutes if she had continued to run. His heart hammered against his chest at the thought.

Without a second of hesitation, she'd put her life in danger to protect her son. He guessed most mothers would do that out of instinct. His mother certainly would not have. His mom didn't even make sure her kid had three meals a day and a warm place to sleep. If it wasn't for Granny—no wonder he felt such a debt to Amy's grandmother. He swallowed hard at the memory of her kindness.

The rattler was a large older snake. The doctor had confirmed that mature reptiles generally had less powerful venom. But he also confirmed that Wyatt had done the right thing by getting her to the hospital as quickly as possible.

What if he had stayed longer at the lumberyard or if he'd accepted his friend's invitation to have a beer?

She didn't even have a working car to drive herself to the hospital. He ran his hand over his forehead to release the tension of a building headache. The rattler had enough venom to kill. Without his help, Amy might have died.

Anger shook him. Now a city girl, she'd forgotten the dangers that lurk on a farm and it nearly killed her. Later, he'd deliver a lesson on dangerous snakes, spiders, and plants to Amy and Bobby. But first, he wanted to see her and know she was going to be all right.

His arms tingled with the desire to hold her, his lips with the need to kiss her and tell her how scared he'd been. However, there was no way in hell he was going to do or say a damned thing like that to her.

Five foot three, one hundred and ten pounds, no matter how motivated she was to handle the job of farming, she couldn't do it alone. She didn't even know how to keep safe. With no money to hire help, it reinforced his belief that she shouldn't try to run the place. Selling was the only option.

A man stood in the doorway of the waiting room, a stethoscope around his neck. He signaled to Wyatt. "You're waiting for Mrs. Long?"

"Yeah." He walked toward the doctor and extended his hand. "Wyatt Cameron."

"John Danelavich." The doctor shook his hand. "Mrs. Long can go home in a few minutes. Make sure she stays off her feet for a couple of days and takes it easy. It might be painful at the site for some time. It will pass. There could be some redness too, but it should be minor. If the site gets worse, she needs to get back here ASAP. But I don't think that will happen. I've told her the same thing. I need someone else to see that she follows directions. I know how people are," he said with assurance. "It's easy to get up too soon, especially with a kid to take care of."

"Yeah. Thanks, doctor."

"No problem. That's why we're here." Doctor Danelavich walked briskly back toward the treatment room.

Wyatt glanced at the sleeping boy and found Sophie sitting in the chair next to Bobby.

"What are you doing here?"

"I came to give you a hand. Doc Danelavich is my cousin. He thought you might need some help."

"Thanks, Sophie." He took a deep breath and discovered he'd almost been holding his breath since he'd arrived in the emergency room.

"They're going to release Amy in a few minutes. Would you watch Bobby while I check with the business office and make sure everything is chill?"

"Of course—go."

He found the hospital billing office and entered. "I'm Mrs. Long's friend. I want to find out if she's okay to leave. She's in the emergency room."

A middle-aged clerk came to the counter. "She's paying with her Visa card. She can go whenever she's ready. There could be more costs to pay later. We haven't had time for a complete accounting."

He pulled out his business card. "If there's any problem give me a call."

"I'll make a note in the file." She stared. "I know you. You're Wyatt Cameron. I saw you on TV."

"Yeah." He got out of the office before she could say anything else.

Sophie was sitting in the same chair when he returned to the waiting room. She was knitting. Bobby slept peacefully next to her.

He nodded to the woman and then gently touched the little boy's shoulder. "Come on, let's get your mom and go home."

"Is she okay?"

"Yeah," he said, relieved. "She's fine."

Amy's foot was bandaged and her expression was tight and her complexion pale when she was wheeled out of the treatment room.

His blood pressure rose and the need to protect her raged in him. "Ready to go home," he asked without showing any emotion.

"You have no idea how ready." A weak version of a smile appeared on her lips. "Sophie, what are you doing here?"

"You don't think I'd miss the excitement. My cousin is the doc here. He called me."

Amy smiled, brighter this time. "Sometimes I forget what a small-town Sierra Creek truly is."

"Well, now that I know you're okay, I'll go and get some dinner ready for you all. Tomorrow, Vanna is going to come to the farm and take Bobby to the daycare center. So, don't worry about anything. Just rest and get better."

"Sophie, how can I ever thank you?"

"Honey, don't be silly." She laughed. "Well, I'm off. Do what the doc said and take it easy."

"I will."

"Shall we go?" The young nurse said as she came to stand behind Amy's wheelchair.

"I—um—please take me to the office so I can straighten out the bill."

"The business has your credit card. They'll call if there is a problem." The nurse started to push the wheelchair toward the entrance. "I have other patients. Let's get you to your car."

"The truck's parked right at the front door." Asleep in his arms, he carried Bobby, toward the exit.

"Mommy," Bobby shouted when he woke while Wyatt was putting him in the truck, joy and relief at seeing her obvious.

Wyatt knew just how the kid felt. Contemplating Amy's death was something he never wanted to think about again. Even now, his heart was racing.

Were the dangers over? Or was the snake the least of her worries?

# CHAPTER 12

**At** the farmhouse, Wyatt insisted on carrying Amy up the stairs to her bedroom. "Get some sleep. Bobby's fine. I'll call you when dinner is here."

"Thanks, but I don't think I could eat." Overwhelming exhaustion settled in her and spread down her back to her sore leg. "Maybe I will take a nap."

"Good."

Moments later, the soundtrack of a children's video played downstairs. She smiled and closed her eyes.

***

When Wyatt came into the living room, Bobby was sitting on the couch watching TV and holding his plush bear.

"I'm going outside to bury the snake. You want to come with me?"

Bobby glanced up at him. "Yeah." He grabbed his stuffed bear. "Can Ted come too?"

"Sure, bring him." He stifled a grin at the cute kid.

Wyatt grabbed a paper bag from the kitchen. He found the snake in the yard and buried it. "That should do." He stamped down the last bit of soil. Bobby stood back clutching his stuffed animal, then he ran to the spot and stomped his feet on the earth too.

"Good job, kid." He gave the thumbs-up sign. "I've got something for you." He held out the rattles from the snake. "They won't hurt you. They're the snake's warning system. Like a car's horn. When you hear that noise, leave the area. Want them?"

"Yeah."

"Good. We'll take the rattles to the house so you can look at them whenever you want to."

"Okay," Bobby said tentatively.

"When I was a kid, I had snake rattles on a shelf next to my favorite toy truck. Come on let's go back to the house."

On the back porch, Wyatt found a canning jar and put the rattles in it. Bobby carried it into the living room and asked Wyatt to put it on the mantle.

Wyatt hoped Amy wouldn't mind. Could be she wouldn't notice.

The rumble of Sophie's old van interrupted his thoughts. She parked, and slowly got out of the vehicle. Carrying a large tray, she went to the back door.

"Hello."

"Come in." He yanked the screen open.

"How's Amy doing?"

"Sleeping."

"The best thing for her. Don't wake her." Sophie set the tray on the kitchen table.

"I'll set out the food and then go. Lots of things to do at home." She held up her hand. "No need to show me around the kitchen. Granny and I spent many hours making meals together here. One of her joys was making food for the church potlucks." She sniffed and wiped her eyes with the white apron she wore. "Where's Bobby?"

"Watching a movie."

"That's nice. I'll take his mind off things."

"I made the dinner from a list of food Amy gave Vanna for the daycare center. Bobby should be able to eat it okay."

"I don't know what you're talking about."

"The little guy can't handle food with gluten in it. Can't digest it, I think. Has to be real careful or he gets sick, vomits and his stomach hurts. It can eventually damage his organs or something. Amy didn't tell you?"

"Not a word."

"Well, can't say I'm surprised. She doesn't want people treating him different. Sometimes people can think less of him and be mean. Of course, I'm not saying you would."

He thought of his childhood with his thrift store clothes and the motel room he and his mother rented by the month. He never belonged, never fit in and was always different. The poor boy with the "slut" of a mother. Yeah, people could be mean, damned hateful.

Sophie set the food containers out on the white cotton tablecloth. "Amy's ex-husband never liked Bobby after he found out he was sickly." She set out three place settings of blue and white Willow Ware plates and lowered her voice. "Soon after Robert learned about his son's illness, he took off for places unknown and without leaving even a dollar of child support for his kid." The woman rubbed her hands on her apron. "Amy's better off without him. That husband of hers was a handsome devil, but he was a nasty cuss."

She adjusted the stainless-steel utensils. "Uh—let me see, there are green beans, beef pot roast and rice. Bobby can eat that all right. I made perogies with cheddar cheese and bacon for you. But don't let him have any. It's made with wheat. That'll make him real sick."

"Thanks. Everything smells delicious. Guess I shouldn't eat the perogies in front of Bobby."

"It's okay. His mama taught him that different people eat different food. He's not quite five and he's little for his age, but he's a smart boy. It's important that he understands some people eat things he can't."

"I noticed he's small for his age, but I had no idea he had a disease."

"Now you take that frown off your face. He's going to be fine. Lots of folks do just fine with celiac sickness. It's lucky they discovered it when he was a baby. If he eats good, he's going to be okay."

"I brought raspberry sorbet for dessert. It's in the freezer."

"Can Bobby eat it?"

"Sure, one of his favorites." She smiled. "Well, got to get going. You take care of my girl."

Sophie was out gone before he could reply.

***

Amy yawned and glanced at the clock, ten in the morning.

Wyatt poked his head in the doorway. "Okay if I come in?"

"Sure. Good morning."

"I thought you'd like a cup of coffee," he said as he entered the bedroom carrying a mug. She brushed

106

her hair out of her eyes and looked at Wyatt, dressed in his usual t-shirt, jeans, and boots. But today he wore a form-fitting black T-shirt that clung to his muscled chest. She tried not to stare. He didn't seem to notice. He was probably used to women watching him.

"You shouldn't have let me sleep so long." She sat up in bed and realized she was still dressed in the clothes she had on when she came home from the hospital. "I must be a sight." She pushed back her tangled hair.

"A wonderful sight. Especially considering what you've been through." His eyes flashed an emotion she couldn't decipher.

"Mommy, look at my book." Bobby ran into the room and jumped on the bed. "Snakes and Spiders of America. We bought it after we buried the snake."

"She groaned and shrank away from him.

"Take it easy. Your mother still has a sore leg.

"Oh."

She scooted over and patted the bed. "Come and show me."

"The snakes are in color."

"Uh—they sure are." She wrinkled her nose as she stared at the black and orange coral snake on the cover.

"Maybe it's too early for your mother. She might want her coffee first. She can read it later."

"Can I watch TV again?"

"I think you better get dressed first."

Bobby ran from the room, slamming the door closed.

"I hope you don't mind the book. We went into town and bought it while you were sleeping. I didn't want him to be afraid of snakes his whole life. Thought the book might help prevent that."

"Well, I—I"

"He needs to know which snakes are dangerous, and which are helpful, and that goes for spiders too. Thought you'd want that, maybe I was wrong."

"No—no." *Bobby needs a man around him.* The realization shook her. She had thought it was enough to parent alone. A man wasn't needed or wanted. Wrong. There were things only a guy could or would think about doing for her son. She certainly wouldn't have bought a book filled with photos and information about poisonous snakes and spiders. "It's good you bought it for him. I'm just being a baby."

"If there's anyone less like a baby it's you." He grinned. "I'd say all woman."

She glanced at Wyatt and her cheeks burned.

# CHAPTER 13

**Wyatt** stepped closer to the bed. "Amy, are you really okay? You went through a lot yesterday."

She adjusted her pillows and leaned back. "Fine, just a little sore. I'll be back on my feet in no time," she said a little too brightly. Chills ran down her spine when she thought of what might have happened if he hadn't been at the farm yesterday. Right in the front yard, she could have died and left Bobby an orphan.

"Vanna will be here in a few minutes to take Bobby to her daycare center. Then he'll go to Sophie's for dinner. Relax, Amy. You don't have to do anything."

"How can I thank everyone?"

"Just get better. You had a close call."

"Yeah." She'd seen the worry on his face at the hospital and he'd taken such good care of Bobby. He must care for her—a little. "I especially want to thank you."

He reached for her hand and held it. She wanted to speak, but couldn't think of anything appropriate. She couldn't say kiss me.

With her hand still in his, she looked into his eyes. Her heart thundered, but she didn't speak.

He sat on the bed and reached for her, pulling her into a gentle hug. She sighed and leaned against him.

Her breathing quickened as he caressed her cheek and then kissed her.

She ran her hand down his back.

He let her go and cleared his throat. "You need to take it easy today." He stood. "Let me know when you want breakfast. I scramble a mean egg."

"Uh—okay." She could feel her face flush. Suddenly embarrassed, she took a drink of the hot coffee he'd brought her. "This is what I need," she said in a strained voice. "I don't want to sleep anymore."

"The doctor said to take it easy." Wyatt helped her put a pillow under her sore leg.

She leaned back. "That's better."

"You should eat something. I'll make the eggs and toast and bring them up."

"Such service."

"Yeah, that's me, one of the best short-order cooks around." He winked and then headed toward the door.

*** 

Amy finished the last bite of breakfast and then sipped her second cup of coffee. "I didn't think I was hungry and I've eaten everything."

"I'm not surprised. You didn't have dinner last night."

He took the tray and put it on top of the dresser that stood near the door.

"There's so much to do on the farm," she said. "I don't like to miss even one day's work."

Without comment, he sat in Granny's boudoir chair near the bed and stretched his long legs out in front of him, his masculinity out of place in the feminine room. "Look, if you are better there are a couple of things we should talk about."

"Oh?"

"While you were still in San Francisco, I contacted a couple of real estate developers and asked them to take a look at the property—just to get an idea of the possibilities."

"But I thought you understood." His words took her by surprise. "I'm not selling."

"It's good to know your options. You see what can happen to a woman alone." He sat up. "Besides, it's too late to call them off. They'll be here this afternoon. Can't hurt to see what they have to say."

How could he be so nice one minute and be such a jerk the next? He was ignoring everything she'd told him about her plans. He was aware of her feelings for the farm. Why mention real estate agents now when she couldn't even walk down the stairs and tell them to get off her property?

"You could have told me about this earlier. Not when it's too late to stop them. I should've known the first day I arrived. Or the next day or the day you kissed me in the barn or yesterday—not now." She heard her voice rise in volume and took a deep breath. She swung her legs out of bed and grimaced.

"Amy, there didn't seem to be a good time to bring it up. The first day you were upset." His eyes narrowed "Where do you think you're going? Get back in bed. Remember the doctor said to keep off that leg for at least a couple of days."

"Don't tell me what to do." She tried to stand and pain shot up her sore leg. "Shit." She sat back down on the bed. "Damn."

"Face it. You're staying in the bedroom today."

"And that pleases you." She glared at him. "This couldn't have worked out any better for you if you planned it. It's clear you want money for your half of the farm and I don't have the funds to buy you out."

Wyatt's expression hardened and his smile turned grim. "I didn't want any of this. I'm just doing what your grandmother wanted."

"That's easy to say when she's not here to back you up."

"Don't."

"Granny loved me and Bobby. She wouldn't want you to sell our birthright."

"Look…"

"You want me back in the city stressing about how I'm going to pay the rent. How to buy food and still keep the lights on? At night I used to go to sleep worrying if I had enough money for gas so I could look for a job and still have enough to pay the sitter?" She scowled at him.

"Finally, the old clunker I owned died and, with no money to fix it, it went straight to the scrapheap. Then I was evicted for being behind on the rent. Bobby and I found our stuff on the sidewalk. If it wasn't for Nan, we'd have been homeless. I'm not going back. I won't. I tell you I won't."

A car honked.

"That must be the real estate guys." Wyatt ran out of the room. The door slammed behind him.

*Damn, Wyatt.* She was shaking and her heart pounded, the memories of living in the city overwhelming her.

She leaned back against the bed pillows. It did no good if she got upset. The realtors were on the farm. Wyatt was the executor of the will and if she pissed him off, he could sell without her permission. Granny always said that you got more of what you wanted with honey than with vinegar.

Amy had to control her anger and try to make him understand keeping the farm was the best option. Could she be sweet to him when all she wanted to do was give him a swift kick in his ass?

She groaned and closed her eyes.

Later, loud voices in front of the house woke her. She strained to hear what they were saying. What was the verdict? Did Wyatt agree to sell the place? Maybe he'd come in and tell her what the agents thought of the place.

Minutes went by, but no one entered the bedroom. Probably for the best, she wasn't up to making nice with Wyatt. Today, she couldn't stomach the thought of another argument. She'd wait to see if he brought the subject up without being asked.

***

Three days later, for the first time since she was bitten by the rattler, she got ready to leave the house. The weatherman promised a hundred-degree temperature by the end of the day. Amy wiped her brow and adjusted her black one-piece bathing suit. And slipped on a grey oversized T-shirt and white shorts. She stepped into her flip-flops and, with a slight limp, went to the kitchen to finish packing the picnic basket, while Bobby looked for his beach towel.

Last night, she'd had a hard time settling Bobby down. He had taken swimming lessons at the YMCA in San Francisco, but he'd never gone swimming in a river. He couldn't sleep because he was so excited.

She had to admit she was keyed up and recalled the last time she'd been to the river with her grandparents. It sent a warm feeling through her.

With the picnic basket and cooler in the back of the truck, she buckled Bobby's seat belt.

"I thought we could go to the Cosumnes River," Wyatt said as he started the engine. "I know a good place to pan for gold and it's a good spot for Bobby to swim."

"Sounds great. I haven't been there since I was a kid. I had a lot of fun then," she said wistfully as she remembered Granny.

After the recent events, they all needed a day off. It was surprising Wyatt had suggested the outing. She still hadn't asked him what the land agents said because she didn't want to start a quarrel with him. Secretly, she hoped he'd been disappointed in their response and that's why he'd said nothing or because he'd considered her position and wanted to please her. In any case, she was going to try honey rather than vinegar with him. When he suggested a picnic, she quickly agreed.

It didn't take long to get to the river. The gently flowing body of water was lower than she remembered but looked just as welcoming as it had when she was a kid.

"Most people use the main swimming hole downstream." He parked on a pullout next to the river. "But I thought this would be a quiet place to pan for gold."

"Perfect." She grabbed the picnic basket and walked toward the river.

Wyatt carried the towels, a blanket and a cooler. He set out the blanket near a picnic table and a barbeque pit.

Amy stood on the edge of the river. She'd taken off her shorts, but still wore her T-shirt. She hesitated. Wyatt's eyes were scanning her. Unconsciously, she tugged on the back of her suit all too aware how out of date and out of fashion she appeared. Dressed like a middle-aged woman, she'd bought the suit when she was pregnant with Bobby. She should have a bikini or at least a two-piece. She put a new swimsuit on her mental list. Unfortunately, with no funds, the list was long and not likely to get shorter.

Wyatt tossed his jeans and shirt on his towel next to the river bank.

Stunned to see him muscled, tanned and wearing only a dark racing Speedo, her mouth opened.

"Mommy, hurry. I want to swim."

She yanked off her T-shirt and threw it on her towel and dove into the water. The cold water filled her big suit. It was just what she needed to cool her heated body after seeing Wyatt.

With her arms out she called, "Bobby, jump to me."

Instead, he waded into the water and squealed with delight.

"Come on, big guy." Wyatt grabbed him and held him in the water. "Use your arms. Bobby, kick. We'll be with your mother in no time."

"I'm swimming. Look."

"Honey, that's great. Come on just a little further."

Unable to wait, she stepped forward and grabbed her son into her arms. "You were super."

"Is that good?"

"Yeah, that's good." She kissed him and turned to see Wyatt grinning at them.

"Amy, is your leg all right?"

"Yeah. All good."

He nodded and swam backstroke to the other side of the river and then with a fast freestyle came back to their side of the river. "It's been too long since I've been here. I can watch Bobby if you want to swim to the other side."

"Thanks."

Afterward, Wyatt took them upriver and, with an old black pan, he showed Bobby how to look for gold.

"Slowly scoop sand and water into the pan and swish it around. Any rock that is heavy, like gold, goes to the bottom. Watch for flecks of yellow. They should be easy to see against the black."

Wyatt filled the pan from the edge of the slow-running river bed and he and Bobby checked for gold.

Amy watched the two of them with their heads together as they peered into the pan looking for sparks of yellow. They were so serious. She couldn't help smiling. She'd never seen her son focus for so long on one thing.

Wyatt filled it again and again and set it down away from the river so Bobby could look through the pebbles, the sun streaming in to reflect anything shiny.

"There's no gold, only a crystal," Bobby whined. "I haven't found any gold all day and I don't want this old rock." He raised his little hand to toss the stone back into the water.

"Wait, don't throw it away. Let me take a look at it. Don't get discouraged. This is our first day. Some of the old miners looked for years before they found gold." Wyatt took the stone.

He turned the rock as he held it in his hand. "Hey Amy, take a look at this. It may not be a crystal. It may be a diamond. They found them here from the eighteen hundred up to the nineteen thirties. But I don't remember anyone finding one in a long time.

"Really? An honest-to-goodness diamond?" She examined it.

"Yep."

Bobby played in the sand uninterested in anything that wasn't gold.

"You think?" She scanned it. "I thought you had to go to Africa to find real ones."

"Not necessarily. California has gemstones too. They did call this area the Mother Lode after all."

"Let's take it home and check it out." She took the rock in her hand, held it to the light and squinted to see it better. "A diamond—wouldn't that be a kick?"

"I don't think they were found in California in the size and quality to make anyone rich like the gold did. Still, a diamond is a diamond. But don't get your hopes up too high. Bobby could be right. It might just be a nice crystal."

"A crystal is good too."

"Definitely."

She held it up to the sun again and turned it slowly in her hand. "Whether it's a diamond or not, I like it. It's not gold, but I feel like one of the forty-niners."

Wyatt laughed and hug her.

If Bobby wasn't there, she'd have liked a longer one.

"I'm hungry." Bobby looked up from his play.

"Kids, always back to the basics." Wyatt laughed. "Okay, let's eat." He took the stone, pushed it into his jean pocket, put Bobby on his shoulders, and walked back to their picnic table.

Amy ran after them.

"We have hot dogs and rice casserole, and freshly made apple sauce." To set a good example for Bobby, there were no chips or beer. She hoped Wyatt didn't mind.

If it bothered him, he didn't show it. "Hmm, good food," he said and rubbed his stomach, then took a bite of his bun-less hot dog. "Eat up Bobby. You have to grow big and strong."

Bobby giggled and rubbed his stomach too and took a bite. "Hmm, good food," he said, his mouth still full of half-chewed hot dog.

Amy couldn't help laughing. "You two kids are crazy." She bit into the food. "Hmm," she said and rubbed her stomach and took another bite of her hot dog. "Good food."

They all roared.

After they ate, Wyatt pulled the picnic blanket out of the hot afternoon sun and put it under an oak tree, while Amy moved the food.

"I want to go swimming again."

"You have to wait at least half an hour after eating before you can go back into the water."

"But Mommy…" Bobby stood with his beach towel over his shoulder.

"Honey, remember it's your job to take good care of yourself. Now that you're becoming a big boy, you have to do what's safe. The time will go fast. You'll see."

"Aw, Mommy."

Wyatt took Bobby's towel and stretched it out under the tree.

She watched her son sit on the towel and read the new book Wyatt had given him, The Forty-Niners, a book written for kids, telling the story of finding gold in California in 1849. It was a relief to have his fascination with snakes and spiders replaced with mining.

With the leftover food back in the cooler, she watched Wyatt pour water on the fire in the barbeque pit.

She'd never met a man so good with kids. It seemed to come naturally to him. Patient, gentle, and enthusiastic, his joy when he was near her son was obvious. It worried her that Bobby took to him so quickly. If she admitted it, she did too. She glanced under the tree. Her son had fallen asleep on his beach towel.

"Amy, come and sit down." Wyatt patted the picnic blanket. "You're working too hard. It's a day off."

She finished folding the red checked tablecloth and sat down next to him. He gently pulled her into his arms.

In the shade of the black oak, a warm breeze played across her face. "It's so beautiful. I'm surprised we're the only ones here."

"The people are probably at the big swimming hole. Amy, relax."

"I'm not good at relaxing. Not enough practice, I guess." She made a halfhearted attempt at a laugh. Her hair must be a mess. She sat up and pulled at her damp hair in an effort to straighten the curls.

"Don't."

"It's so curly."

"Curls are sexy." He took her hands from her hair and pulled her against him again.

"If I'd known that I wouldn't have spent half my life trying to straighten them." Nervous, she giggled.

"You have no idea how sexy you are. Do you?" He kissed her when she started to answer. Slowly, his tongue played with her lips until she opened them for him.

When his tongue entered, fire shot through her and the hot summer breeze seemed cool in comparison. Her breathing quickened as he caressed her and when his attention slid to her breast and he rubbed her nipple with his thumb, she moaned.

# CHAPTER 14

**A** shiver went down Amy's back as Wyatt caressed the nape of her neck and then left a trail of hot kisses on her skin. His hand closed around her tightened nipple.

Again, she realized how she hungered for Wyatt. She'd wanted him since her crush in high school. Did he know? Had he seen the desire in her eyes?

With her eyes closed, she tangled her fingers in his hair and then worked down to his muscled back. She heard his intake of breath as she reached his backside.

He sent his tongue to probe her open mouth as he played with her breast, kneading and pulling until she wanted to scream with pleasure.

Carefully, he helped her lay down on the blanket. Her body tingled, and her breathing was fast. Her hips arched up searching for his touch.

His mouth found hers again and she opened for him. Unexpectedly, a vision came to her. Wyatt was telling her the real estate agents were on the farm looking it over for a sale. Was the farm already on the market?

"Stop." She sat up. "I don't know what came over me."

He gazed at her, an unreadable expression on his face. "What's wrong?"

"I—not in front of Bobby." She adjusted her swimsuit, better not to start a disagreement in front of her son. No point in ruining his day. "It's late. We better get Bobby back to the farm."

Wyatt frowned. "Amy I…" He glanced at her son and then shrugged. "Whatever you say."

He picked up the sleeping boy from the towel and put him in the cab, then quickly packed the truck.

No one spoke on the way home. Even after Bobby woke, he was silent. Perhaps he sensed the tension and thought it was best not to talk.

She still tingled from Wyatt's touch. Was she drawn to him because of her high school fantasy about him? She considered it. He was gorgeous. Any woman could see it, but he was an interloper, a man with plans that made it impossible for her to complete her life goal of living on Granny's beloved farm and passing the land on to her son. Bobby needed to understand there were only two in their family, everyone else was temporary.

***

Two days had gone by and Wyatt hadn't spoken to Amy since they left the river bank. That was for the best because he wanted her. The longer he thought about it, the more he understood it was wrong.

They had different agendas. Traveling all over the country following the rodeo circuit as he intended to do again, the last thing he needed was an entanglement with a woman and a kid. He was free and wanted to stay that way. He had to remember that when a pang of hunger for Amy growled in his insides.

Since she didn't complain, each morning he rode with Bobby. It surprised him how much he looked forward to seeing the boy. Though he was small for his age, it pleased him that Bobby took to riding, improving each time he rode.

Against his will, he found himself watching Amy when she didn't notice, his need to protect her increasing. At the same time, his desire to see any other woman decreased. *Shit.* Nothing made sense because he didn't want a permanent relationship with any woman, especially not Amy. He shook his head.

He drove his truck, the bed filled with lumber, to the broken-down corral on the farm. The four-by-fours had shifted in the bed when he pulled to a stop and parked. If he calculated right, there should be enough wood to rebuild the corral.

In a couple of days, he could get the job done assuming his back held out. He stretched and rubbed the sight of his injury. It had nearly healed. There was no reason not to return to the circuit. *Not yet. I can't leave Amy now.*

The gas engine posthole maker thundered in his ears. The muscles of his arms shook as he controlled the machine. Just one more hole to go and there'd be enough. The ground was softer than he'd thought and surprisingly free of rocks, probably because Amy's grandpa had prepared the ground for the corral years earlier. Nonetheless, it was tough going. The sweat drenched his jeans and the t-shirt he wore clung to him. He removed his shirt and hoped for a breeze.

"Hey."

Wyatt spun around to see who was talking. "Wes, what are you doing here?" He watched his brother come toward him from the direction of the farmhouse.

"Amy told me you were here."

Wyatt reached out and shook his brother's hand.

Wes grabbed him and turned him so he could see his bare back.

"That's one hell of a wound you got. It's almost the perfect shape of a hoof. Bro, you must have made that horse real mad."

"Yeah, well you should see the horse." He grinned.

"Seems like you were the one who got messed with, buddy."

"It's nothing. All healed." He picked up his shirt and pulled it on to cover the injury. "So, what brings you all the way out here from the state capitol?"

"Just driving by and thought I'd stop in."

"You never were good at lying. Cause highway eighty-eight is right on the road to nowhere. Find another excuse. Don't you have anything better to do?" He tossed a hammer at Wes. "Since you're here, pick up the hammer and join me. We'll have this corral built in no time."

"Kind of hot for work, don't you think?"

"Well, good to see you, Wes. If you can't give a guy a hand, I got work to do. Why don't you get back to Sacramento?"

"Wyatt, wait. Okay, I did have a reason for coming up here. You're not going to like what I have to say, but listen before you tell me to get the hell out of here."

# CHAPTER 15

**Wyatt** set his hammer down on the ground and stared at Wes. "Spit it out. Why are you here?"

"When are you coming back to the rodeo circuit? Everybody's wondering."

"When I'm ready."

"Hell, you look ready now. If you can do this kind of work, you can sit a horse. What's keeping you?" Wes paused, then said, "Your sponsors are wondering why you're not riding."

"Did they send you up here?"

"They just told me you haven't answered your email or text messages. There's talk around the circuit that you can't cut it anymore. You're hurt more than you admit and you're getting old."

"You're serious?"

"Damned right, Wyatt. You had a good thing going. But remember no one stays on top forever and once rumors start—the sponsors are worried. They want to see you. But only if they are getting the best cowboy possible."

A chill ran through Wyatt. It had to be ninety degrees in the shade, and yet he felt cold run down his spine. "I've always given a hundred percent. No one's ever paid me for something I didn't deliver. I've got the championship belts to prove it. Damn, I haven't had a day off in almost two years."

"Hey." Wes held up his hand in a defensive move. "Don't kill the messenger. I'm just saying the sponsors are concerned. They want you back on the circuit winning or they're going to find someone else."

"Who? You maybe? You planning to take my spot?" Wyatt threw lumber from the truck bed. "Why did they send you out? Why not call me?"

"They have. You don't answer your damned phone or return the messages they leave."

He grabbed another four-by-four. Wes was right. He hadn't even charged his phone in a couple of weeks. "If that horse had kicked me any harder, I'd be in a wheelchair right now. It didn't, but that doesn't mean I don't deserve time to recover."

"Then call and tell them. Wyatt, get them off my back. Give them a date when you can work."

Wyatt jumped from the bed of the truck, picked up a post and dumped it in one of the holes he'd dug. Then he rotated his shoulder. "I just need a little more time."

Wes took off his cowboy hat, swatted a fly and plopped the hat back on his head. Then he exhaled loudly. "We both know what you're thinking about and it's not going on the circuit."

"Get it out, Wes." He let go of the beam he was holding and glared at his brother. "Just say it."

"Charlene tells me you don't come around anymore. But she sees you in town with Amy and her kid." He swatted another fly.

"Shit. You could have any woman you want. Is playing house with a divorcé that much fun? My God, she isn't even all that pretty. Look at her. She's scrawny. Next to Charlene, there's no comparison. And Amy's got someone else's kid."

"Wes, don't go there."

"Ready to give up your career and Charlene? You going for the librarian type now? Is mousy the new "turn-on" or is she easy? Is that it? She opens her legs for you anytime, anywhere?"

Reflex action, Wyatt felt his fist hit Wes's jaw before he knew what he was doing and could think better of it.

His brother was spread eagle on the ground, eyes big and his lower lip swelling.

"Damn. I'm sorry, Wes. But you don't know Amy." He offered his hand to help his younger brother up. "If you did, you wouldn't say something like that."

Wes stood without help. "Don't let her ruin your career. Go back to work before she wrecks it for you. Get there while they still want you." He brushed the dirt off his jeans. "She must be an awesome piece of ass for you to act like this, but she's still just a slut."

A woman gasped. Wyatt turned to see Amy standing behind them, a jug of water in her hand. A shocked expression spread across her face as a tear ran down her cheeks.

"I didn't mean for you to hear that," Wes said, sheepishly.

"Amy," Wyatt reached for her.

She dropped the water jug, turned, and ran.

"Wait." He watched her dash toward the farmhouse. She stumbled, almost fell, caught herself, and continued to run without looking back.

"Get the hell out of here, Wes," Wyatt growled through his clenched jaw, fury running in his veins.

His brother started to speak, stopped, and walked away.

***

The farmhouse was quiet when Wyatt entered. Bobby was still at daycare. Amy sat at the kitchen table with a bowl of apples and a paring knife. Her eyes were red, her skin pale.

"My brother didn't mean what he said. He's a stupid kid."

"Wyatt, I remember him from high school. He's a year older than I am."

"Really? He seems younger."

"It's not only what he said. Now I understand how it looks to people with you living here. People must think that we are—uh, you know. They think what your brother said."

She picked up an apple and stared at it. "They wouldn't say it to my face. Until your brother said it, I guess I never thought about how things appeared to the people of Sierra Creek. Maybe I lived in a big city too long. Everyone is pretty anonymous there."

"Sometimes Wes is an idiot. Don't take what he said seriously. You know we've never done anything to be ashamed of."

"I know, but Bobby and I have to live in this town. I'm his mother and I need a good reputation for him and the farm. I can't be the slut who runs the organic apple farm."

He recoiled from her words.

She tossed the apple back into the bowl. "You've done enough to keep your promise to Granny. No one could ask more of you."

128

She pushed her eyeglasses out of the way and rubbed her eyes. "Wyatt, I've been selfish. I wanted your help. Bobby needed you, but we're okay. It never occurred to me that helping on the farm could hurt your job. I didn't realize that while you're here, your career is at a standstill and your income has stopped. I don't want that. I—I don't want you to stay. You can leave."

"Amy…"

She left the room.

***

Early the next day, Wyatt spent a couple of hours tuning Granny's old Volvo. He fired it up and the old workhorse purred. He'd made an appointment at the service station to get new tires, realignment and balancing and have new brakes installed.

When he left the farm, he'd have the peace of mind knowing, in case of another emergency, Amy and Bobby would have a safe car to drive. His heart thundered at the thought of either of them needing medical care again.

Last night, he had finally checked his messages and found his brother was right. Both his boss and his agent sounded damn pissed that he hadn't bothered to return their calls. He'd better get in touch with them or he might be looking for a new career.

His only excuse for not calling sooner was that after his accident he wasn't sure he wanted to go back on the circuit. Lying in bed in pain, he wondered what would make a relatively smart man, with a college degree in business, take the kind of risks he took just to entertain an audience who probably didn't give a damn if he was hurt, as long as they got a thrill.

At some point, the money wasn't a good enough motive. Fame sure didn't mean anything. In fact, it was an annoyance. So why did he do it?

It might be time to do something with his degree. Was he ready to settle down and sit behind a desk? Could he picture himself pushing paper all day and be happy to do it or would he be bored out of his mind?

He slammed the hood of the Volvo down harder than he meant to. He didn't know what he wanted to do. And the confused emotions he had for Amy weren't making things any easier.

His body hardened at the thought of her. He wanted her. If that was all he needed, he could take her and move on as he'd done with so many other women. But for the first time, he didn't just want sex. He needed more from her.

She was constantly on his mind, getting in the way of his usual thoughts. Until recently, worry had been a stranger to him, but now it was a constant companion. Gut-churning concern for Amy and Bobby pulsed in him. The sooner he left and got back to his old ways, the quicker his life would return to normal. He'd go back to the party circuit as well as the rodeo circuit. Yeah, that was the answer. Get out of town—ASAP.

\*\*\*

The weather changed as September neared its end, the days not nearly as hot and the nights cooled. October's crisp weather would be there soon. Amy noticed the leaves were changing color. Her favorite season of the year, but this time it was difficult to enjoy it. The stress of making ends meet and the need to be sure the farm succeeded was pulling at her.

It was hard to believe it had only been a few weeks since Wyatt left to go back on the rodeo circuit. Without him, the days went by slowly and even the fall colors seemed grayer, duller. It was her fault because, against the advice of her friends and her good judgment, she'd fallen in love with him.

From the desk in the den, she glanced out of the window to the backyard cottage and the sign Bobby and Wyatt made together. Her son missed him too. Daily he asked when Wyatt was coming back. She was becoming good at avoiding answering the question. After all, she couldn't tell him what she didn't know.

There'd been no word from Wyatt. She hadn't expected any, but had hoped he might send a text or an email for Bobby.

Her son talked about horses and said when he grew up, he was going to be a cowboy just like Wyatt. Thankfully, kindergarten had started and he was now busy making new friends. After a while, he would forget about Wyatt and move on. Wouldn't he?

With the horses gone, the only thing that caused her to believe Wyatt might return was the costly exercise equipment gathering dust in the corner of the barn. Or maybe, he'd send a moving company to pick it up.

With too much pondering and no answers, she turned her interest back to the computer screen. Granny's Organic Apple Farm website was finally up and running. She'd been pleased that the local women had proudly shared their family apple recipes and allowed her to put them on the website with their names and photos proudly displayed next to each recipe. Her favorite was the apple butter recipe.

Each day, she learned information that could help with the running of the farm. Articles on the internet talked about the care of organic apples and how to nurture the organic soil. She learned about diseases and bugs that could attack apple trees. More than she ever imagined existed and she tried not to be repulsed by the information about creepy crawly critters. After all, she was a farmer now.

Manny Gordon, the man whose crew harvested her apples, was waiting for an order of additional trees for the north orchard to be planted next spring. He offered to lend a hand to get the soil ready for the new plants. Though he'd cut her a good deal, she still had to make sure the money to pay him was available when the time came.

In a short time, the pumpkins would be ready to pick. She and Bobby had nurtured a special pumpkin they hoped would win the "Biggest in the County Contest" at 4H. They couldn't cut it for a jack-o'-lantern. Every day he watered the pumpkin and checked to see if it had grown any larger. With the rain coming, soon he wouldn't have to work so hard.

Today, she was setting up a Facebook page to talk about the farm's maze and pumpkin patch for Halloween and Thanksgiving and had taken to tweeting every day. If she could entice families from Sacramento to visit the farm during the holidays, might return for a Christmas tree in December. At least that was her hope.

Of course, nothing would happen if she couldn't get the hay bales out of the driveway and to the field to form a maze.

Jonathan Hansen, the man whose farm bordered hers, had brought the bales to her and they littered the driveway. However, moving them into the field and making a maze proved to be harder than she'd thought.

*If Wyatt was here, he'd know what to do to get them in shape. Stop. Grow up and learn to depend on your own ingenuity.*

She'd proclaimed to Wyatt she could run the farm. Well, it was time to do it, the moment to prove she could manage things. She had to set an example of success for Bobby.

She rushed out the back door and almost ran into the cord of wood near the bales of hay in the driveway. She'd forgotten she ordered the wood to prepare for winter. The oak logs waited to be stacked in the wood box on the porch and it needed to be done before the rains came and soaked the logs.

No matter how tired she was, later tonight she'd have to work on the woodpile. She glanced at her hands. Her nails were broken and her hands were callused.

A decision about repairs on the chicken coop had to be made too. If she wanted to raise free-range chickens and sell the eggs it would have to be fixed soon. The chickens needed a warm place to roost when the cooler weather returned.

Why had she thought she could manage this farm on her own? She needed a handyman. No, what she needed was Wyatt, but he wasn't here, He never would be. Even if he came back, he wouldn't stay. To him, a wife and family were a burden to be avoided.

*\*\*\**

A warm breeze raked over her as she wandered up a dusty road to her neighbor Jonathan Hansen's farm. With her sneaker-clad foot, she kicked a clump of dirt out of her way. Could she keep her nerve and ask Mr. Hansen a question? A simple request for assistance from anyone had always been difficult for her. Even as a kid, she didn't like to ask for help. Her desire to do it by herself was always foremost in her mind.

A small wooden, ranch house appeared in a grove of Ponderosa pine trees. With a deep breath, she walked up the front steps and knocked on the door.

No answer. After several knocks, she wandered around the farmhouse and saw a fenced enclosure. Mr. Hansen, in his makeshift barnyard, was tending to his goats.

A lanky man with grey hair and blue eyes, she couldn't guess his age, but he carried his body with the strength of a man still in full command.

He smiled when he saw her and brushed the dust off his jean coveralls and blue work shirt. "Mrs. Long." He bowed slightly.

"Hi, Mr. Hansen, nice day we're having."

"How are you doing with that maze of yours?"

"Um." She paused, surprised by his question, apparently not a man to make small talk. "Well, I— that's what I came to talk to you about."

He wiped his snarly hands on a blue bandana. "What can I do for you?"

"I see you have a tractor and I was wondering—" Amy hesitated. If she phased it wrong, she'd lose the help she so badly needed. "I, uh—"

"Spit it out, girl."

# CHAPTER 16

**Mr.** Hansen's voice sounded sharp, but his eyes remained kind, a smile still on his face. "What do you want?"

"I could give you free-range eggs if you help me get my hay bales into a maze. I don't have any money, but I'd give you as many eggs as you want."

He waved his hands in the direction of his chicken coop. Then he wiped his brow with his bandana and put it in his back pocket. "Do I look like I need eggs?"

"Well, I—"

She could feel her cheeks burn. Without another word, she turned and walked away.

"Don't run off," he shouted.

She stopped and looked back at him.

"You give up awful easy. If you're gonna be a farmer, you can't quit at the first sign of trouble, cause farming is nothing but trouble." He winked.

"Oh."

"Now, Mrs. Long, like I said, I got lots of eggs. But I don't have any apple pie. Since my wife, Lucy, died a few years back, I've had none."

"I'm so sorry to hear of your loss."

He rubbed his hand over his mouth. "I'd sure fancy some homemade pie."

"You know I've lots of apples and I can make pie. Even if you can't help me move the bales, I'd be pleased to bake you an apple pie. Of course, I know it won't be as good as your Lucy's pie, but I'll do my best."

"That's good enough for me. I'll bring my tractor down to your place tomorrow morning and move the bales to wherever you want."

"Thank you, Mr. Hansen. Thank you so much."

"Call me Johnny. All my friends do."

"Johnny, I'm Amy to my friends." She grinned and offered her hand.

He hesitated, cleaned his hand on his jeans again and then took hers. "Nice to make your acquaintance, Amy."

***

Just after she returned to the farmhouse, Amy's smartphone rang. "Hello."

"Are we going to meet at the ice cream parlor at noon today?" Vanna asked.

"Yeah. Does that still work for you?"

"It's fine. My teaching assistant will cover for me at school. That should give us enough time to talk before you have to pick up Bobby from the after-school program."

"Great. See you."

She glanced at the regulator clock in the den, enough time to shower and dress. She should wash her hair, put on make-up, and open a new box of contact lenses, but if she did, she'd be late.

***

When Amy arrived at Sophie's ice cream parlor, dressed in old jeans and a new white T-shirt, Vanna shouted hello from the table near the window.

"Hey," Amy joined her at the table. "Vanna, is that a new phone?"

"Yeah."

"I finally got my mom to get Wi-Fi at the shop."

"Let's see if we can connect."

"What do you want to look up?"

Amy started to tell her, but Vanna was already typing in Wyatt Cameron's name in the search engine. "Bet you'd like to know what he's doing."

"Vanna, not here."

"No one's looking over our shoulders." Her friend laughed.

Amy had never told anyone, but she'd followed Wyatt's progress on the rodeo circuit online. She was glad he'd recovered from his injuries and was winning again. No one seemed able to stop him. Even his brother wasn't successful against him.

"Look, Amy, here's a photo."

She glanced at Wyatt's smiling face. Too often, in photos, he had a gorgeous woman on his arm when he accepted one award or another. In this picture, he and an unknown brunette grinned at the camera.

"Amy."

"Yeah. I see it." She tried to sound uninterested as she stared at the gorgeous woman next to him. What had made her think he'd cared for her? For an intelligent woman, sometimes she was stupid, damn stupid.

"I wonder who she is," Vanna said.

Amy watched Vanna scroll down and saw several photos of Wyatt with different women on his arm.

"I don't know, but there sure are a lot of them." Amy yawned and hoped her voice had just the right amount of boredom in it.

"You can quit yawning. You don't fool me, Amy McCarthy Long. I know you want him," Vanna whispered in the crowded shop, "you told me how much you miss him. Admit it?"

"I won't. What's so great about him anyway? I don't get it."

"Uh, well, let me see. He's single, tall, handsome, and rich. Oh, and he likes kids. Yeah, I don't get why women like him either."

"Enough."

"Okay, Amy, you don't want to talk about him, all right," Vanna said. "You want a diet cola?"

"Sounds good. As far as Wyatt is concerned, I haven't heard a word from him since he left. So, it doesn't matter how I feel. He wants Charlene."

Vanna wrinkled her nose. "She's not in any of the photos. There's a different female in every picture. And none of them are Charlene. She must be an old story. Out of the picture, so to speak." She grinned.

"Somehow, that doesn't make me feel better. He's got a lot of women after him and I'm not about to be just another one in a long line of females wanting Wyatt Cameron."

"Liar, liar pants on fire." Vanna laughed.

Amy giggled. "You've got to get away from the daycare kids. You sound just like them."

"I know. Isn't it pathetic?"

They both laughed.

"I'll get the colas," Vanna jumped up from the table, heading toward the counter and then ran quickly back. "Look who just walked in," she whispered and sat back down at the table.

Amy glanced at the front door in time to see Charlene, wearing red leather pants and a matching waist-length jacket, saunter on her four-inch black heels into the ice cream parlor.

She tossed her long black hair back and even from where Amy was sitting, she could see the woman's perfectly manicured red nails and painted lips. She was dressed to flaunt her beauty.

Amy might have found her amusing if she weren't now feeling under-dressed and unfeminine in comparison.

"Sophie, sugar, get me a diet Coke with a drop of vanilla to go please," the woman purred.

"I'll get our drinks." Amy got up before Vanna could and strode to the counter. "Hi, Charlene."

A lack of recognition spread across her face. She squinted then said, "You're the apple girl. Aren't you from Granny's farm?"

"Amy."

"Where's that darling little boy of yours?" She continued without glancing at Amy. "Is his daddy back from San Francisco?"

"We're divorced."

"Oh." Her eyes narrowed and her smile faded. "Wyatt belongs to me. Keep your dirty stubby little hands off him."

Unconsciously, Amy glanced at her own callused hands and then back at Charlene's manicured fingertips. "I have no claim on him." She hesitated. "And from what I've seen, neither do you."

"You little witch," Charlene hissed. "If I were you, I'd consider your reputation, especially with Wyatt living on your farm. For your little boy's sake, I'd be careful who you piss off. It doesn't take long for a *nasty* rumor to start in a small place like Sierra

Creek." The woman grabbed the paper cup so hard it looked as if the drink might explode over the top.

"Back off." She leaned toward Amy. "Wyatt's mine. I won't warn you again." The words squeezed out between her nearly perfect white teeth.

"I…"

Charlene marched out of the shop.

The wave of feral cat behavior shocked Amy. *I must have hit a nerve.*

"What just happened?" Vanna asked when she returned to the table carrying the drinks.

"No idea. Guess I've gotten under her skin."

"Maybe she's seen the photos of Wyatt with all those women and when he's home, he is staying on your property."

"Vanna, don't look at me like that. We are living in separate buildings. He's in the cottage. Anyway, if she's been watching him on the internet, she can see I'm not in any of the photos."

"Yeah, but neither is Charlene. She can't get to the other women, but you're here. Wyatt probably said something nice about you and it set her off."

Amy took a sip of cola and considered her friend's words. "Maybe he said something nice about Bobby. They get along really well, but not about me. I've been nothing but a pain to him. He had a promise to keep and as executor of Granny's will, he has a job to do. That's all."

"If he likes you, don't push him away. You say you don't *need* a man but…"

Vanna's phone went off. "Yeah, oh sorry to hear that. Okay."

Amy watched her friend nod, then Vanna disconnected. "Laurie isn't coming. Her car broke down and she's waiting for the tow truck. We'll have to reschedule our get-together."

"Is she okay?"

"Yeah, but disappointed."

"Me too. I was looking forward to seeing her. You know, getting the high school crew back together." Amy slumped in the chair.

"I can't say I'm surprised the car broke down. It's hard to believe Laurie has kept that old clunker going for this long. Her husband lost his job when the mill closed. Going on two years now."

"That's terrible."

"Yeah. He does odd jobs but is still looking for steady work. I guess a lot of the men in town are. If something doesn't come up soon, we'll lose a lot of good people. They'll be forced to move."

"Is that why she's so excited about crafting for the farm's pumpkin patch?"

"They sure need the money." Vanna paused. "Oh, did I tell you, she's pregnant again?"

"No."

"How far along is she?" Amy asked, remembering the excitement of finding she was carrying Bobby's and pushing down the memory of her husband's reaction when he said he didn't want children.

"She's about three months, so still a little queasy."

"Ugh, I remember that."

"If she makes money with her crafts, it will be of some help."

Amy glanced at the regulator clock that hung on a nearby wall. "We could flesh out some ideas for the pumpkin patch and update Laurie later. I think there's still time."

"Great." Vanna crunched a piece of ice.

141

From her back pocket, Amy grabbed a piece of computer paper and flattened it on the table. "I've drawn an idea of the maze. See." She turned it toward her friend. "Johnny Hansen is making it. He'll have it done in a few days."

She took a quick breath. "If you can help the little kids choose pumpkins in the patch and Laurie can bring their crafts, we'll sell them. I'll have apple and pumpkin pies for sale. Naturally, there will be jars of apple sauce and bottles of apple cider." She took a quick breath. "If we had a little more time, we could have a haunted house for the middle school kids." She shrugged. "Maybe next year."

"Wow, girl, you've certainly thought this out. How about having picnic tables and we serve the kids and parents pieces of pie and apple cider right there on the farm? I'm sure we could borrow the tables from my preschool."

"I love that. I'm getting pumped. I so want this to work. Vanna, remember to tweet and share."

"I will. It's going to be a success."

"Hi, Amy." A male voice called.

She looked up expecting to see Wyatt.

Mike Donnelly, the manager of Sierra Creek's largest grocery store, stood grinning at her.

"Hey, Mike. What are you doing here? You like Sophie's ice cream?"

"You got me." He laughed. "I'm sure it's great, but I buy mine at the grocery store. I just saw you sitting in the window and decided to come in and say hi."

"Sit down," Vanna said.

"Thanks." Mike sat down in the chair next to Amy.

Vanna winked at her.

Amy kicked her friend under the table and cleared her throat. An awkward silence began.

"Oh, I didn't realize it was so late." Vanna stood up. "I'll call you tonight. Got to go. Bye."

Amy grunted. There was no way she wanted to be alone and try to make "happy talk" with Mike.

His shoulders relaxed and he leaned back in the chair. "So, you all settled in now?"

"Pretty much." She finished her cola, making a slurping sound with her straw and resisted the inclination to grab an ice cube and pop it in her mouth.

"Uh, how's your little boy?"

"Fine."

"He's a cute kid."

"Thanks."

"Sierra Creek's a good place for a kid to grow up."

"What? Uh, yeah."

Not exactly a sparkling conversationalist, but she couldn't think of anything to say to Mike. Why was it so hard to talk to him when it was so easy to chat with Wyatt?

"Amy." Mike waved his hand in front of her eyes. "You still here?"

"Oh sorry." She forced an imitation smile to lift the corners of her mouth. "You going to get something to eat?" She nodded toward the ice cream counter.

"Can't. Got to get back to the store. I came in to tell you I've been thinking about you."

# CHAPTER 17

**"You've** been thinking about me?" Amy noticed the dimple in Mike's cheek as he grinned at her.

"Yeah. A lot. Remembering you when we were in high school. I had one hell of a crush on you then."

"I didn't know."

"Never told you. I watched you back then."

She felt her cheeks redden. He'd always just seemed one of the guys in her group. Nice enough, but she'd never really paid much attention to him. "High school seems like forever ago."

"A long time and yesterday, if you know what I mean." He suddenly looked serious. "Come to dinner with me on Friday night."

"Uh. I don't know. I have Bobby to take care of." She looked down at her hands and hoped he'd understand she was saying no. "I don't know if I can get a sitter."

"Come on, Vanna can babysit for you or Sophie can. I'll ask Sophie right now if you want me to." He started to stand.

"No. Okay. I'll go to dinner with you." She paused. "But I'll get a sitter."

"Okay. I'll pick you up on Friday at seven. See you."

She tried to smile. "I guess," she said under her breath, but Mike was already gone from the ice cream shop.

He had rushed out as if he wanted to leave before she could change her mind.

*Damn, what have I done?* Guilt churned in her stomach for agreeing to go to dinner with Mike. Open and friendly, he deserved someone interested in him.

For days, Wyatt was the only man she thought about. But Mike wanted to take her out. And from what Sophie had told her, Mike wanted a wife and lots of kids. He wasn't running from a permanent relationship. That was more than she could say about Wyatt. With annoyance, she thought of the many women he had on his arm in the multiple photos she had seen online.

Bobby needed the influence of a man. But Wyatt didn't want the responsibility. Why not let Mike have a shot?

Still, she already regretted her decision to go to dinner with Mike. If she was going to be fair, Wyatt was the man she wanted, but she'd have to go through with the date because she'd promised and she would keep her word.

***

Friday night came too quickly. In Bobby's room, Amy grabbed his pajamas from under the pillow on his bed. "I'm going to dinner with a guy from the grocery store. I met him in high school. I know you'll have fun at Sophie's house. You can have sorbet and Vanna promised to play a board game with you before you go to bed."

"Okay." Bobby grabbed his teddy bear off the bed and put it under his arm. Then he took his book on snakes and put it under his other arm. Will Sophie read me a book before bed?"

"Yeah. I think so if you say please. But why don't you bring another book too and let her choose the one she wants to read." Amy cringed at the thought of Sophie opening the snake book and seeing the color photos.

Can I bring The Teddy Bear Says Good Night book?"

"Perfect. I think that's one of Sophie's favorites." Amy relaxed, relieved.

"Mommy, someone is knocking on the door."

"That's probably Mike. Come down and meet him."

"Can I bring my books and my bear?"

"Of course." She kissed him on the cheek.

He wiped his cheek and said, "Mommy, you smell good."

"It's the perfume I got for Christmas last year. Thanks, baby."

"Aw, I'm not a baby."

"I mean big guy."

Bobby grinned.

**\*\*\***

Amy opened the front door and found Mike fumbling with a paper bag.

"Hey." He smiled. Dressed in dark slacks and a white long-sleeved shirt, he looked like he could go back to work at any moment.

"Come in."

She held the screen door and he entered. Bobby stared at Mike and she realized the man was taller

146

than she remembered. He must look huge to Bobby, though in her mind he was much smaller than Wyatt.

"Hey, kid." Mike held a hand out to Bobby.

Her son pressed closer to her and squeezed her leg.

"Aren't you going say anything to Mike?"

Bobby stuck his thumb in his mouth and stared.

Mike cleared his throat. "I brought you something. Instead of flowers, I got a bag of oranges for you, good vitamin C. I mean you live on an apple farm, so I thought you might like a change—these were on sale." He frowned. "Stupid I guess."

"No. It's very uh—original. Bobby and I love oranges. And you're right, being on an apple farm we haven't had any in ages." She grinned and took the bag. "I'll just put them in the kitchen. Bobby, why don't you show Mike your book?"

"Do you have a horse?"

"No. Can't stand the smelly animals."

"I like horses." Bobby stomped his foot. "They're nice."

Amy heard the conversation from the kitchen and quickly rushed back to the living room before Bobby could say anything else. She was just in time to see Bobby step closer to Mike.

"Want to see my book?"

"Okay."

"This is my favorite one." Bobby handed Mike the book with the page open to the color plate of the poisonous snakes.

"Get that away from me." Mike knocked the book from Bobby's hand.

Bobby screamed.

Amy ran to pick up the book.

147

Mike's face reddened.

"I don't like him." An expression of disgust spread across Bobby's young face. "Can I go to my room?"

"Good idea. I'll tell you when Sophie gets here."

He ran upstairs.

"Don't like snakes much." Mike shrugged and rubbed his hand over his chin.

"I don't blame you. My history with them hasn't been a happy one. But I don't want Bobby to be afraid of them."

Mike frowned.

*Well, this meeting went as well as a train wreck.* She remembered how Bobby and Wyatt had connected the first time they saw each other. *Don't go there.*

"I think I hear a car." She hurried to greet Sophie.

*It's going to be a very long evening.*

***

Mike held the door open to the Italian Village Restaurant. "The food's great here. The best Sierra Creek has to offer. But not as fantastic as you look tonight." He grinned.

She might have scoffed, but she saw by his expression, he meant what he said. Self-consciously, she adjusted the strap on her green tank top and smoothed her short multicolored skirt. "Thanks. It's been a long time since I've dressed up."

"You should do it more often."

His glance, as he scanned her body, chilled her.

Quickly, she walked into the restaurant. The aroma of freshly baked pizza and red wine greeted her. People's voices and Italian folk music mingled pleasantly in the room. Though dimly lit, she saw the hand-painted scenes of Tuscany that covered the plaster walls. People sat at the red and white cloth-covered tables. Lights from the twinkling candles, set in the middle of the tables, sent shadows flickering on their smiling faces.

"Hey, Mike," a forty-something maître d' said. "Saved a good table for you."

The man pulled out a chair for Amy at a table much too close to the dark corner of the room. She noticed the man winking at Mike before he left. "Your waiter will be here soon," he tossed the words over his shoulder as he returned to the front of the room.

After they ordered, Amy leaned back in the chair a sipped her glass of Chianti. The wine warmed her and left her feeling less tense. Mike was finishing his second glass of wine.

"So, how do you like working at the store?" she asked, trying to be polite.

"It's good." Mike perked up. "If I play my cards right, I'll have a job for life."

"Wow. Not many people can say that in this economy. You're lucky."

"Yeah. I worked in retail when I was in high school. After I graduated from Sac State, I came back to Sierra Creek."

She tried to look interested.

He kept talking, explaining the ins and outs of the grocery business. She responded, "Yeah." at what she hoped were the appropriate times. She admired his enthusiasm for his work. Though he was a nice guy, she was having trouble raising any passion for him.

Many women would love to be at an expensive restaurant having dinner with a single, employed, good-looking guy. And he was paying for the meal. Why wasn't she pleased?

As Mike continued, the premonition of a long night loomed again. She suppressed a sigh and pushed down the wish to be at home reading a nighttime book to Bobby.

"The margins are small. People don't know that." Mike's voice raised in volume. "Everybody has to eat. Right? They see the store congested with people and assume we're making a ton of money. But that isn't necessarily true. You have to buy right. Produce goes bad and so does milk and yogurt. It's not as easy as you might think to run a store."

"Well, I—"

"Your vegetarian lasagna." A young waiter set a dish in front of her. "Careful. It's very hot."

"Thanks. Smells wonderful."

She took a bite and swallowed. She could eat the mouthwatering wheat pasta without worrying that Bobby could somehow taste it and have a reaction to the gluten.

Mike ate his mashed potatoes, meatloaf and mushroom sauce, talking between bites. He never once asked her a question about herself and showed no concern about how she was doing or how things were going on the farm.

When she couldn't eat more, she took a sip of wine. Mike had eaten everything on his plate and had exhausted his monologue on the management of a grocery store.

Now, he was spouting statics about the San Francisco Giants Baseball team and the memory of the day he got drunk when the Giants won the World Series in 2010. Presumably, he wasn't aware of when the Giants won the 2012 World Series, because he made no mention of those games.

She glanced up and found him smiling, but not at her. His warm grin was for his memories. The sound of his voice became white background noise. She even gave up nodding appropriately. He didn't seem to notice if she did or not.

Freed from the responsibility of answering or responding to his babble, she relaxed and gazed around the restaurant and took another sip of wine. How romantic the restaurant would be if she were with someone she cared about, like Wyatt.

A young couple at the bar were kissing, "necking" as Granny used to call it. She watched. Not polite to gawk, but she couldn't seem to stop.

Movement in a dark corner caught her eye.

"Wes, you've had enough to drink."

*Wyatt.* The words sent a chard of pain running through her. She squinted to see further into the corner.

"Come on, let's get you out of here. That's right Wes, stand up."

She watched Wyatt drag his brother to a standing position. It was too dim for Amy to see if he was embarrassed by his brother's behavior, but his voice was composed.

He was back in town. She would not have known he was in Sierra Creek if she hadn't accepted the dinner invitation from Mike. She felt a sting and her chest tightened. He could've at least let Bobby know.

"Bro, I need another drink."

"You've had enough." Wyatt took a deep breath.

Wes swayed and moved into the main part of the room. She watched as he came closer to her table. Wes sagged and Wyatt pulled him up right.

"You're doing fine. Keep moving."

"Amy, you slut, you ho." Wes stopped at her table and glared. "What are you doing here? You're not good enough to be in a respectable place like this."

Conversation in the restaurant stopped and the people stared at her. The silence grew. A waiter stood frozen, holding a tray of hot food. He gaped at her, as did the rest of the people in the room.

"I won't let you destroy his career. Leave Wyatt alone, bitch."

She gasped.

Wes lunged at her. Wyatt grabbed him. "That's all, buddy. Get out!" he growled.

Wyatt's eyes met hers. Even in the low light of the restaurant, she could see his blue eyes flash, but she couldn't read the emotion in them. He helped his brother navigate his way out of the restaurant.

Her back crawled. The customers were still staring and she realized Mike was as well.

"What the hell was that about?"

"Uh." Amy shrugged. In order not to make eye contact with any of the other patrons in the room, she looked down at her plate.

Slowly, the buzz of normal speech returned to the room, the sound of silverware being used and the tinkling of glasses could be heard.

"Can't stand a man who doesn't hold his liquor." Mike drank the last drop of wine and burped. "Watch who you get involved with. You have your boy to protect. This isn't San Francisco." He set the empty glass on the table. "Let's get the hell out of here."

Amy bristled at his advice, but she bit her tongue. She wanted to tell him to get his mind out of the gutter and show her some respect. But there'd been a scene in the restaurant tonight, there didn't need to be another.

The ride back to the farm seemed longer than usual. Mike didn't speak. She tried, but couldn't think of much to say to him that wouldn't start an argument.

In the driveway, he turned off the engine and glanced at her, his expression serious. "Amy, I'm a plain-spoken man and I have simple plans for my life, marriage to a good woman, and a big family." He looked her in the eye. "I've had a crush on you since high school. I've thought about you—often. Maybe I let my fantasy of you get out of hand, but I expected more from you. You let me down."

"Mike, I…" Suddenly cold she rubbed her arms.

"You're a handsome woman. I'll admit that. Damned attractive, but you have a different way— you have loose rules and you live with Wyatt. Tonight, I realized I need a woman—let's just say someone who is less complicated."

"Not a slut."

"That's not what I said. But if the shoe fits… I live quietly. I'm a traditional man. There is nothing wrong with that."

"No." *You're just an old-fashioned traditional jerk.*

"If you ever need help finding anything at the grocery store, I'll help you, but—" He turned the engine back on.

It was her signal to leave his car. No walking her to the front door. Not that it mattered, but he had proclaimed he was an old-fashioned gentleman. He should walk a lady to the door. *Oh.* The message was clear. In his eyes, she wasn't a lady, only a fallen woman giving out favors to Wyatt. *Good grief.* She was sitting next to a dirty-minded dinosaur in the body of a young man.

Her throat tightened and for a moment she fought tears of anger. Mad that she'd wasted an evening and had been made a spectacle by people she didn't even like.

As soon as she was out of the car, Mike gunned the engine of the compact vehicle and speed away. She was left to fumble in the dark for her key. She entered, slammed the door and leaned against it. *All men are jerks.*

She changed into a short pink nightgown but was too angry to sleep. In the kitchen, she brewed a pot of decaf coffee.

The front doorbell rang. She glanced at the old wall clock that hung near the stove, damn near eleven o'clock, too late for a caller. *Bobby.* There must be something wrong. She ran to the door and yanked it open.

# CHAPTER 18

**Wyatt** filled the doorway of the old farmhouse and was silhouetted by the moon.

"I parked down the street. I didn't want to wake Bobby."

"He's staying with Sophie."

"Oh." It was hard to read his expression as he took off his cowboy hat and held it in one hand. "Look Amy, I don't apologize very often." He hesitated. "I'm sorry about what happened at the restaurant. Wes was way off base."

"Well, let's say I won't be going back to that eatery anytime soon." She could feel her cheeks burn. "Wyatt, it wasn't your fault."

"I feel responsible."

"I'll live."

"Let me come in."

"You can go back to the cottage with a good conscious." She heard the hard edge of her voice.

"I don't know what's wrong with Wes. Too much to drink, I guess. There was no call for him to treat you like that. Sometimes he's an ass."

She crossed her arms in front of her chest and glared at him. The air had turned cold and she shivered as the wind blew through the open doorway.

"Amy, you're cold. Let me come in before you catch your death…"

"I'm fine right here."

"I had no way of knowing you'd be at the restaurant with Mike or that Wes would behave badly."

"You thought I'd be sitting home alone, waiting for you."

"I just didn't expect to see you. Invite me in."

"Like I said, it's late.

"Let's talk."

"I'm tired."

"Offer me a drink."

"I don't have any liquor, no beer."

"I don't want booze. Make me a cup of coffee, or decaf or—hell, I'll even drink tea. I just want to talk."

"Really?"

"Yeah?"

"Amy, I thought we were pretty good at conversation."

She sighed. "Okay, you win. Come in and I'll cut you a piece of apple pie and you can have some decaf. Then you have to leave."

The short pink nightgown hit her thighs when she walked. His eyes were on her. She could feel the heat of them burning her backside. If only she hadn't changed into her night clothes.

In the light of the entryway, she pushed her glasses up from her nose and scanned him. Maybe it was the comparison to Mike, but he seemed taller, tanner, and more muscled. There was a new intensity in his expression, making him even more appealing.

"How are you? Are you actually all right?" He cleared his throat and stared at her.

"Yeah." Her voice sounded unsure even to her ears.

"Amy, I've tried, but I haven't been able to stop thinking about you."

Was that supposed to be a compliment? He wanted to forget her but couldn't.

She sure wasn't about to tell him she thought of him too.

"Go into the living room. I'll get the pie and coffee."

"I could start a fire."

"Okay."

In the kitchen, she took a deep breath. Wyatt was the last person she expected to see. Her heart pounded. Confused emotions swirled in her. Why was he here now of all times? What couldn't wait until tomorrow when she'd be more composed? And why, tonight of all nights, had she chosen her shortest nightgown to wear?

The two cups and saucers rattled on the wooden tray as she carried it to the living room. She set the tray on the table in front of the sofa.

The fire was burning in the fireplace and Wyatt was putting the fire screen in place.

With a sigh, she sat down and watched the flames. He sat on the couch next to her, nearly touching her. She resisted moving away. Instead, she sipped the hot decaf, letting it slide slowly down her throat.

"Hey, the pie's pretty good."

"Thanks." She tucked her leg under her and watched as he took the last bite of the apple pie and set his empty dish and fork on the table, then picked up his cup.

"No pie for you?"

"I couldn't eat anything."

His eyebrows lifted, but he didn't ask why?

"How's Bobby?"

"Good." She smiled. "Loving school." She set her cup on the table. "Uh—if it's okay. I mean—how is Wes? If you don't mind my asking."

"He's drunk as a skunk and is going to feel like shit in the morning. Couldn't be more deserved."

"Oh."

"Don't know why he's meddling in my life. We didn't even grow up together. As you probably know, he went with my father and I stayed with my mom after the divorce. Now he's acting like my father instead of my younger brother."

Wyatt was explaining. Something he'd said he never did. Why?

"I've changed, Amy. Could be I'm getting old." He sat up and searched her face. "I thought I couldn't wait to get back on the circuit and to the endless parties, and the drinking. Now that I'm there, I'm thinking how good it would be to come home from work and talk to someone who listens to me. I want to sit on my own couch, put my feet up, and watch my big-screen TV. Only, I don't have a television, no couch. I don't even have a home." He laughed without humor.

"Where do you live when you're not here on the farm?" She'd been wondering but never had the nerve to ask.

"Wherever my suitcase lands, a few days here, a week there, then a few days somewhere else. I follow the rodeo circuit. Granny's farm is the closest thing I've ever had to a real home since my mom died. That never bothered me—until now."

"I know your parents were divorced, but what about your mom's home? Didn't you live with her when you were a kid?"

"When she settled down after the divorce, she rented a one-bedroom apartment on Main Street above the meat market. You could say I bunked at her place. I slept on her couch when she let me, if she didn't have a "gentleman," as she called them, staying with her. Too often she did and needed her space, always looking for a man to love her. She never found one." He hesitated. "Died alone."

Amy watched him stare at the fire, his eyes were cold and unmoving, pain etched in his expression.

"What about your father?"

"Out of the picture," he growled. "Took my brother and left town. I learned later that when my parents divorced, they each chose a son. My dad didn't want me because I looked too much like my mom. She opted for me. I was older and less trouble." He shrugged and finished his decaf.

She waited for him to continue, concerned if she spoke, he'd stop sharing.

Finally, he said, "I can't count how many nights I stayed with kids from school. I'd stay until their parents got sick of having me around. Tired of an extra mouth to feed." He rubbed his forehead as if the memory hurt.

"When I didn't have anywhere to stay, I slept in the park. That's what got me in trouble. Granny caught me one night and gave me what for."

He smiled for the first time since he'd arrived. "You knew her. She was a little bit of a woman, not more than five feet tall. Still, she said she was going to whip my butt if I ever stayed all night in the park

159

again. She would have done it too." He chuckled. "Long before it was popular to say it, she believed that it took a village to raise a kid."

"I can just hear Granny promising to spank you?" Amy grinned. "What are you about six feet?"

"Yeah, but I saw the fire in her eyes. She meant what she said. From then on, she made it her mission to be sure I had food and a warm place to stay. She found a way of doing it without embarrassing me. It was our secret. She never told anyone what she did and neither did I—until tonight."

"You cared about her?"

"Loved her." He cleared his throat.

Amy sighed. Granny must have loved Wyatt too. "My biggest regret is Bobby won't grow up knowing her like we did."

"He'll learn about Granny from you. I bet you've got a hundred stories you can tell him."

"I hadn't thought of that. I might even write stories down for Bobby." She leaned closer and kissed him on the cheek. "Thanks."

He looked startled, but then he reached out and pulled her into his arms and kissed her, gently at first, then with increased power.

Her arms went around his neck as she opened her mouth to permit his tongue to enter. It danced with hers.

With his fingers, he massaged her shoulders, slowly releasing the tension. She let her head fall forward and he moved her hair out of the way and placed kisses on her neck, sending a shiver of longing through her.

With ease, he rotated her so she faced him. He pressed his lips on hers again. For a moment, there was only the crackle of the fire, his hands stimulating her, and the sound of her rapid breathing that increased with his continued touching.

"Amy, I missed you these last few weeks. You were in my thoughts because I wanted you near me."

His warm breath played across her cheek just before his mouth took hers again. She moaned with pleasure. The realization that he longed for her sent hope spiraling in her. She gasped, "Yes." as he fingered her breast and increased the intensity of his kiss.

He pulled away. "I said we'd talk. Only talk." His voice was husky and his breathing rapid. "You feel so good it's hard, but I'll keep my word."

"I want you, Wyatt. You must know I do. With her hand pressed against his chest, she felt his heart thundering.

"Yeah, Amy."

"Wyatt, it's just—I can't do a one-night stand. I'm not made that way." She watched the light from the fire make shadows dance in the room.

"I know." He ran a gentle hand against her cheek.

Suddenly cold, and sitting near him, she was tempted to share the night with him, even if it was only once.

She shivered. "I have a responsibility to Bobby. I couldn't look at you the same way if we—you know. He'd sense things were different between us." Was she telling Wyatt or did she need to hear the words out loud to give her strength?

"Amy, I'm not pressuring you. Relax and let's enjoy the fire."

His arms flexed and held her gently to him. She pressed against him, her head on his chest. With a sigh of contentment, she closed her eyes.

"Tell me your stories of Granny," he coaxed.

"Well, I guess my first memory is the day I arrived in Sierra Creek. I came by bus carrying a small suitcase and a ragdoll named Molly tucked under my arm. My mom, like yours, wasn't cut out for motherhood." She paused.

"To be fair, at seventeen my mom left the farm and went off with a man she thought loved her. By eighteen she was on her own, a single mom, and overwhelmed by the prospect of raising me alone. She tried for a few years. I'll give her that." Amy gulped for air. Glad Wyatt continued to hold her gently to him.

"Mom couldn't support me, but she didn't want to come back to the farm. When I was six, she sent me here by myself." Fear ran through her as she remembered. "I'd never met Granny. Of course, I knew she was my grandmother and I was going to live with her. But I was terrified."

She snuggled closer and he stroked her hair.

"When I got off the bus, Granny was waiting for me. She hugged me and said, 'Come on baby, you're home now.'" Amy gulped back a sob.

Moisture filled her eyes and she blinked. Now that she'd started talking, she couldn't seem to stop telling stories about her grandmother's temperament, her love of the farm, and how Granny adored Grandpa. She shared things that only Wyatt could appreciate.

He listened without a word, an intense expression deepening the lines around his narrowed eyes.

"This is the first time since her death I've talked about her without crying."

With a quick wipe of her eyes, she said, "Tell me your stories."

As she listened, they both laughed and she wept, but it was a good cry. And the whole time he held her.

The embers in the fireplace burned low and dawn was breaking when he left. With a nod and a wave, he walked out of the farmhouse.

When would she see Wyatt again?

# CHAPTER 19

**It** had felt right to let Wyatt hold her. The corners of Amy's mouth turned up remembering. Still, her rational brain told her it was wrong.

They both loved her grandmother. Understanding that sent a wave of relief coursing through her. But even with their similar experiences, by way of Granny, they'd come to very different goals. He cared about the farm, but he could sell it. She couldn't.

Though he said he wanted something else, his career made sure he'd always be on the move, a free agent responsible for no one but himself. She, on the other hand, had formed a family unit and had Bobby to consider in all her decisions.

How could she love a man who, in the name of helping her, wanted her to sell Bobby's legacy and destroy her dream of self-reliance and financial independence? Was love and hate interchangeable? With a groan, she closed the front door.

Somehow, she'd stop Wyatt from selling.

\*\*\*

The sun rose as Wyatt reached his truck. He got in the cab, but didn't start the engine. Instead, he recalled Amy's kiss. Sweet, sincere, and different from any he'd shared with other women. Not only that, last night he'd talked more to her than he'd ever spoken to anyone.

There was a vulnerability about her that let him feel safe telling her things he'd never shared. She'd listened without expressing judgment and he'd conveyed things even his brother didn't know.

He rubbed his stiff neck and stifled a yawn. The cottage had a bed where he could flop. No. It was too close to the farmhouse and Amy and his desire to have her. He imagined her in bed, sexy, and wanting him. He recalled the feel of her body pressing against him. His need hardened. The cottage was too near to her.

He'd told her he only wanted to talk. He lied, not merely to her but to himself. He wanted to take her and make her his. He shook his head in disgust. She and Bobby deserved a family man with roots in the community and a stable job that allowed him to come home every night, not a cowhand with wanderlust and an uncertain future. She needed someone like Mike.

No matter how much money Wyatt earned, as he got older, he was still going to end up just another broken-down cowpoke. He started the truck's engine and drove away.

***

The next morning in the farmhouse's driveway the rumble of machinery caught Amy's attention. She wiped her hands on her cotton apron, ran to the kitchen window, and looked out. Wearing jean coveralls and a blue work shirt, Johnny Hansen sat on his tractor, straw hat on his head, ready to move the bales of hay just as he promised. Not many men in her life kept their word. *Thank you, Johnny.*

At the back door, she leaned out and yelled, "Hi Johnny, come in and have a cup of coffee. I've got breakfast cooking, eggs and bacon."

"I appreciate the offer, but I ate. If you don't mind, I'll get started. If you show…

Bobby ran up to the door and peeked out His eyes widened when he saw the man and his machine. "Can I ride on the tractor?" he interrupted them.

"When you're older, Bobby."

"Aw."

She tousled his hair "You'll grow up fast enough." With his small hand in hers, she walked out to speak to her neighbor.

"Johnny, I've got a picture of what I hope the maze will look like." She took a folded plan from her pocket and showed it to him. "I wondered if we could do something like that. I thought we could put it in the meadow next to the house. But not too close to the berry patch." She paused.

Johnny ran his gnarled hand over his stubble-covered chin, but didn't speak.

"Uh. That way it's near the pumpkins and the barn where we're going to have the refreshments and the crafts." She handed the plan to him.

He wiped his brow with a blue handkerchief and pulled the plan close to his face. "Can I keep this?"

"Sure."

He stared at the paper for a long moment. "Yep, I can do this." He waved the paper in the direction where she wanted the maze. "Show me exactly where you want it and I'll put it there."

"Oh Johnny, that's wonderful." She wanted to hug him but was afraid it would embarrass him.

166

While he moved the hay bales, Bobby helped her clean the tack room next to the barn.

"We're going to use this room for the craft shop," she said. "Over there in the corner, we can set up tables and your friends can have pie and apple juice."

"I like apple juice. It's my favorite." Bobby set the broom he was using against the wall, coughed and wiped the dust off his jeans. "I like it better than orange juice."

"Yeah, me too." Amy laughed, remembering the gift Mike gave her. "But they're both good for you."

She glanced around the room. "Now that the stuff is out and we've cleaned it, the room is bigger than I realized."

"Was I a good helper?"

"You were great." She hugged him. "We'll have lots of room for tables and chairs so everyone can sit down and still have enough room for shelves to put the crafts on."

"Can I play now?"

"Okay, but stay close to the barn where I can see you. I'll be here painting. And keep an eye out for snakes."

"Gee, Mommy. I know about snakes."

"I just worry." She drew him into her arms and hugged him again. So small and delicate, she doubted strangers would guess he was nearly five years old. *Please, God, keep him safe.*

He pulled out of her arms and ran into the yard. So grown up and that's what she wanted. But soon he wouldn't want her hugs, because he'd be too big for that kind of stuff.

With the broom, she yanked down the last cobweb and opened the can of paint left over from

Bobby's room. She could hear him playing in the yard. The sound of Johnny's tractor buzzed in the background, the hum of a busy farm. The life she'd dreamed of was becoming a reality.

Three hours later, she stopped to take a break and get lunch ready. She glanced at Granny's old wristwatch, one o'clock. "Late for lunch," she mumbled. Bobby was still playing in the yard with his cars.

"Time for lunch. Go wash up."

She'd heated the beef and carrot stew she'd made earlier and tossed a salad. In the morning, she'd baked two apple pies, one to eat and one for Johnny to take home. The kitchen still smelled of baked apples. She breathed in slowly and then exhaled. *Nothing better than the aroma of baked pies.*

Where was Wyatt right now? What was he doing? Was he thinking of her? She shook her head to clear it. *He has a long line of women he could be thinking about. All prettier and with fewer problems than you. So, stop.*

After he left this morning, she'd promised not to mull over their situation, no point in tormenting herself. It was crazy wishing for a relationship with a man who had more women in his life than anyone she'd ever met. No matter how much Bobby needed a man's influence, it wasn't fair to let him care too much for Wyatt. A man who didn't want to be her son's father.

He was probably on his way back to the rodeo circuit and this time she wouldn't follow his travels online. A grown woman shouldn't waste time dreaming of a relationship that could never be.

There was enough to do with taking care of Bobby and the farm, including the pumpkin patch and the apple orchard and the blog talking about farm life. The more she concentrated on getting those things right, the better chance she had of keeping the property.

A man like Wyatt only brought emotional upheaval to her life and she certainly didn't need that. Decision made. She'd forget about any future with Wyatt. She grabbed a quick breath and relaxed her shoulders. She and Bobby would be just fine on their own.

"Honey, did you wash your hands?" she shouted from the kitchen doorway, looking toward her son's room.

With the table set for three, she went to find Johnny and tell him lunch was ready.

She got back from the meadow and entered the house in time to see her son open the front door. "Honey, where are you going?"

Bobby ran out of the house to the front porch.

It was then she heard a pickup truck in the driveway.

# CHAPTER 20

**She** glanced out the living room window just as the black Ford F150 rolled to a stop.

"Hi Wyatt," Bobby yelled.

"Hey, big guy."

Her heart thundered as she watched Wyatt jump out of the cab. Bobby ran up to him.

"Where's your horsy?"

She couldn't hear the answer because the sound of Johnny's tractor drowned out their voices.

Bobby waved his hands in the air as he talked. Wyatt leaned down and then he kneeled on the ground near her son. Her boy's expression became serious. Wyatt leaned closer. There they were speaking man to man. Again, she was reminded how much a man's influence was needed.

The noise from the tractor stopped and she heard Wyatt say, "I've got something for you."

"For me?"

"Yeah." He went to the cab of the truck. "I got a new book for you. It's about dogs, all kinds of breeds, how they look and what they do."

Amy saw the excitement in her son's eyes as he clasped the new book to his chest.

"How'd you know I needed a doggie?" He ran to the front door where she was standing. "Mommy, look what Wyatt gave me."

"That's wonderful. Did you say thank you?"

"Thank you," he said and ran into the house.

"You didn't have to do that."

"I wanted to. It'd be my fault if he went around scaring half the town with his snake book." He grinned.

Amy's heart thundered. Damn, Wyatt and his charming grin. She had just prepared herself for not seeing him again. And now here he was unsettling her and her son. Anger raced through her, but it quickly changed to joy when he smiled again.

"I didn't think I'd see you—so soon, or ever."

"Thought you and Johnny could use some help with the maze."

"Guess we could," Johnny agreed.

Wyatt moved toward her and she felt his strong presence, his manliness barely leashed. He said the right things to her, but there was an undercurrent radiating from him. An emotion she wanted to decode. She looked up. He was staring at her.

"Uh, we were about to have lunch. Why don't you join us?"

Bobby ran out of the house still carrying the new book. He grabbed Wyatt with his free hand and pulled him toward the farmhouse.

She noted a look of reluctance in Wyatt's expression. He shrugged and walked toward the house.

At the kitchen table, Bobby's eyes glistened with happiness as he talked.

When the old man entered the kitchen, Wyatt said, "Hey, Johnny."

"Cowboy."

She watched the two men shake hands. Then the guys fell into easy conversation as she served the meal. Soon, they had the paperwork for the maze out on the table and were discussing the best way to proceed and get the job done.

Her son watched them with rapt concentration.

How long would Wyatt stay? A day? A week? Not long enough for a five-year-old. That was for sure. In a while, Wyatt would be back on the rodeo circuit, making nice with his many women friends, and grinning for the cameras. She and Bobby would be left alone, again.

*I won't let Bobby fall in love with Wyatt—like I have.* Her son had already been abandoned by his father. Could he deal with a loss of a second man in his life? Would he come away thinking he'd done something wrong or worse yet, think he wasn't loveable? A small hiss escaped her lips.

"Amy, did you say something," Wyatt asked.

"No—more pie anyone?"

"I'm good." Johnny shook his head. "Let's get back to work. Now that you're here, we'll make good time."

"I'm right behind you."

Johnny walked out of the room. The screen door shut tight after him.

Bobby ran from the kitchen with his new book held close. Amy started to clear the table.

Wyatt took a dish from her hand. "You smell good, all beef stew and apple pie." He reached out and drew her to him. With his rough hand, he gently

172

pushed her hair back from her face and bent down, his mouth hovering near hers. He searched her face as if wanting to find affirmation of her desire before he kissed her.

About to speak, her lips parted and he kissed her. A playful contact as his tongue danced along her mouth then plunged deeper to strengthen their touch.

The sway of her body moved with his as he lengthened the kiss and his hand moved to her breast. A tingling sensation sent a wave of yearning racing through her. Without conscious thought, she rolled her hips to meet his and pressed against him. "Wyatt," she whispered.

"I want you Amy," he groaned. "Need you, but not here, not now."

He set her free and she stumbled back from him. She flushed and the heat burned her cheeks.

"I know we can't, but I couldn't leave the kitchen without a taste of you. I've got to help Johnny. Later today, after he goes home, I have something to tell you."

Before she could respond, Wyatt was gone.

**\*\*\***

That evening, Wyatt watched Amy come out of the farmhouse onto the front veranda. She'd changed from her work clothes and she now wore a sleeveless white cotton dress that hugged her pert breasts. The hem touched the top of her knees. She carried something in her hand.

"A baby monitor," she said as she set it on a small table next to Granny's old rocking chair. "I can hear Bobby if he needs me." She sat down in the chair and crossed her legs. "He wanted to sleep with the book you gave him. I had a hard time convincing him to take a stuffed animal instead."

Wyatt chuckled at the image.

"I can't believe how much you and Johnny did in one day. The maze is wonderful. I'm getting excited. I hope people will come to the pumpkin patch." She sat back and rocked slowly in the antique chair.

"They'll come." He leaned against the railing.

"How can you be so sure? I've been tweeting about it for days. I made a Facebook page. Vanna gave me photos of kids in costumes and I put them up with photos of the pumpkin patch. I've even included a photo of Bobby's pumpkin. The one he's growing for the "biggest" pumpkin contest and I'm still worried no one will show up." She sighed. "I'm rambling. You know I do that sometimes."

"It's okay." He sat in the rocking chair next to hers.

In the light of the full moon, her hair shimmered.

"It's so beautiful here," she continued.

He knew she had no idea of her beauty.

"I can't explain how content I feel living here on the farm. Bobby's happy too."

The words hit him like a fist to the gut. Granny had been so sure Amy hated the place and wanted to sell the place. As the executor, if he forced the sale, he'd hurt Amy. Or would he be keeping the farm with all its inherent problems, from putting her financial security at risk? He groaned.

"Are you okay?" She stopped rocking and sat up in the chair.

"Yeah."

"Wyatt, would you like a beer? Or I could make some iced tea or decaf if you're thirsty."

"I'm good." He tried to relax and let the night air cool him. He had something to say to her and the longer he waited the harder it got.

An owl hooted as a slight breeze rustled the trees near the house.

With reluctance, he said, "Bobby told me something today. I think you should know. Now don't get too worried."

# CHAPTER 21

**Amy** gasped. "What's wrong with Bobby?"

"He told me something "man to man," but I thought you should be aware of it."

"Tell me."

"He's having a problem at school."

"Is this what you meant this afternoon when you said you wanted to talk to me?"

"Yeah." He could see the disappointment on her face.

"I thought it was about—I mean—never mind."

Had she expected a commitment from him?

She cleared her throat. "What's wrong at school? Bobby said everything was fine when I asked. He was making friends."

"He is, but some of the older kids are teasing him. They make fun of him because he eats "funny" food. They offered him cookies and he wouldn't eat them. That pissed the kids off. So, yesterday they grabbed his lunch, called it garbage, threw it in the trash, and laughed at him."

"That's not funny. Why didn't Bobby tell me?"

"He didn't want you to get upset. Like you are now.

"I—"

"He's trying to be a big kid."

"Did he tell his teacher?"

"No way. The kids said if he told anyone, they'd throw him in the trash along with his food."

"Oh God, I'm stunned. I know kids tease. I remember being called "four eyes" because I wore glasses. That hurt my feelings, but I was never threatened physically.

"You're a girl."

She threw an odd look at him, stood up, walked to the porch railing, and held on to it. "With celiac, I've been so careful about his food, and so proud he knows what not to eat. This is serious. It could have terrible repercussions if he goes off the diet. I have to tell the school administration."

"Bobby wants to handle it."

"Yesterday, he came home crying because his stomach hurt. Now I understand why. This can't go on. I have to talk to the school."

"He came up with an idea and I promised I'd tell you."

She spun around to face him. "Wyatt, he can't do this without me. You need to understand that he's small and frail for his age and will never be tall or strong like you."

"Amy, you've got to stop thinking of him as a sickly kid. He's okay. You can't follow him around his whole life. Let him take a few chances and make a mistake or two. That's what makes a man, regardless of how tall he grows."

"You don't understand."

"It's all right to be small in stature as long as he gains self-confidence. Maybe you don't see it, but your kid has the heart of a lion. Let him try. You can always step in later if he can't do it. Don't take this opportunity from him."

"Me? I'm not taking anything away from him. I'm not the one making his life miserable at school." Her voice rose. "Since he was born, I've done everything I could to protect him. Bobby *was* a sickly baby. I watched him struggle to survive. You didn't hear him cry all night when nothing worked to soothe him. What do you know? You weren't there the night he almost died. You can't know how terrifying that was. It's *so* easy for you to preach." Tears ran down her contorted face. Anger flashed in her eyes.

"Amy…"

"Don't." She glared at him.

He wanted to hug her, but a gut feeling told him it would only make things worse. "You're right. I can't know the pain a mother goes through," he said quietly. "I *do* know what it feels like to be a boy without a dad to show him the way, a guy who instinctively wants to be a man. It's a struggle to make the right choices without a dad's example."

He stepped closer and caressed her cheek. "Let Bobby try. Give him some slack to fight his own battles. He'll survive. And he'll love you for the opportunity to start becoming the man he wants to be."

"He's so little," she whispered.

He reached for and held her. "I know, but trust me. He'll be all the stronger for this."

In his arms, her body trembling against him, she sobbed. "I want to do the right thing."

"Amy, it's going to be okay. Sit down and I'll tell you an idea Bobby and I came up with to fix this."

She wiped her eyes and returned to the rocking chair.

"I don't think the kids who took Bobby's lunch are bad." He watched her frown, unconvinced. "They felt insulted because he wouldn't eat their mom's cookies."

"But they threatened him."

"I'll give you that the kids overreacted and they scared him. Still, when it comes right down to it, all they did was talk." He smiled thinking of her son speaking to him this afternoon.

"Amy, you've got a bright kid. He's proud of his food and knows you're a good cook. He got the idea to share lunch with the kids at school, so they'd see how great it tastes."

He paused to let her absorb the suggestion.

"Anyway, I thought why not bring food for the whole school? Then everyone would know about gluten-free and try some of it. You'll have to prepare it. Say hot dogs and the rice casserole you made the day when we went to the river for a picnic."

"Bobby was so happy that day." She hesitated. "Do you think taking food to school would help?"

"Yeah. What boy or man, for that matter, can resist a tasty meal?" He chuckled. "And you're an excellent cook. The kids would like it. Some organic apple sauce would be great too."

"I could do that."

He watched her body relax as she leaned back and smiled at him.

"Vanna is friends with Bobby's teacher. Maybe she could talk to his teacher and see what she thinks of the idea," Amy suggested. "That way, Bobby could fix this without being a "mama's boy.""

"A good thought."

"Wyatt, I think this might work."

In the moonlight, he could see her frown had disappeared.

"I'm so grateful for your help."

A soft breeze stirred the night air on the veranda and she crossed her arms around her body.

"Amy, you're cold."

"I'm fine."

"You should get some sleep. Bobby will probably be up early."

"Yeah. He's an early riser. Where are you staying tonight?"

"I thought I'd use the cottage. Do you mind?"

"That's okay. Uh—can I join you?"

For a second, he thought he hadn't heard her correctly. "What did you say?"

"Let me come to the cottage with you." She paused. "Wyatt, don't you want me?"

Even in the dim light, he could see her eyes widen and her lips pout.

"You know I do. But I can't offer you forever."

"Forever," she scoffed. "I had a promise of forever from my ex-husband, Robert. You see how that turned out."

As she came closer to him, he could feel her body heat and smell a wisp of her floral perfume. To his surprise, she sat in his lap and drew his face to hers. "Please," she whispered. "Pretty please."

He kissed her and the sweet taste of her sent a jolt of hunger through him. He moaned and glanced down and saw her nipples tighten against the thin fabric of her dress, begging for his attention. With one arm he scooped her up and with the other arm he grabbed the baby monitor.

He walked to the cottage and once inside, he kicked open the bedroom door, put the monitor on the bedside table and gently set her on the bed.

# CHAPTER 22

**In** the dim light, Amy watched. Wyatt stripped off his shirt from his expansive shoulders. His abs were even more defined than she recalled, her fingertips tingled as she imagined touching him. Heat flared as she scanned him from his handsome face to his taut chest and powerful legs. He pushed down his blue jeans and boxer shorts in one movement and stood before her wearing only his grin.

"Whoa." She sucked in a quick breath as she noticed his manliness growing.

"Your turn." He smiled.

Anxious, she trembled. She sat up and pulled her dress over her head, then tossed it to a nearby chair. "Wyatt, it's been a very long time," her voice cracked. "Since I've—I've—I haven't been with anyone for—" Breathless, she stopped.

He joined her on the bed and touched her lips with his fingertips. "It's okay."

With shaking hands, she undid her bra and lay down.

He slid her pink bikini underpants down and dropped them to the floor. She covered the jagged scar just below her abdomen.

"What are you hiding?"

"I had a cesarean with Bobby." She'd always been embarrassed by the mark of her failure to deliver her baby in the "normal" way.

"Don't hide. You brought a wonderful boy into the world. You're beautiful just as you are," his voice cracked with emotion.

A shiver of anticipation ran down her spine. She caught her breath when he bent down and tenderly kissed her.

At that moment, she realized she'd never known the engrossing passion that now pulsed through her. It overwhelmed her. She pulled him closer.

His body hovered over hers, almost touching, while he eagerly took her mouth. Her breath quickened as he suckled at one breast and then the other. He stroked her curves with a delicate touch.

She let her hands roam over his expansive back and down to his tight buttocks.

He found her core and probed it until she wanted to scream his name. Instead, she opened her legs to him. Her hips surged upward, searching for his entry, delighting in the pressure of his hard body on top of her as he filled her.

"Ah, Ah," she cried as she found release, her body tingling as sensations spread from her core to radiate outward even to her fingertips.

With one final driving force, Wyatt pierced her, a low groan of completion signaling the release of his seed into her.

For a moment, she couldn't think or speak. Her hammering heartbeat and the sound of her jagged breathing pulsed in her ears. *I Love you, Wyatt.*

"You're amazing," he said in a husky voice.

Entwined with him, his strong arms enfolding her, she sighed and rested her head on his broad chest. With a smile, she closed her eyes and relished the feeling of him. Her heartbeat began to return to normal, but Wyatt's warmth continued to surround her.

When she was married to Robert, she had sex. But with Wyatt, she made love. For the first time in her life, love filled her.

Naked, she lay next to Wyatt and smiled.

**\*\*\***

Somewhere in the distance, a rooster crowed. Wyatt opened his eyes to the early morning light that pierced the partly open shade of the cottage's bedroom window. A sense of well-being meandered through him as he stretched. With his eyes closed again, he allowed himself to enjoy the memory of Amy making love to him, her body moving with him while he filled her. A yearning for her sent a pulse of heat coursing through him.

Even before he checked, he knew Amy was gone from his bed. It was a good thing because if she'd been there, it would have been beyond his control to stop from having her again.

In the past, when he'd had sex with a woman and she was gone in the morning, a sense of relief had filled him, glad he didn't have to deal with her after his appetite was satisfied.

Loneness fought to the surface of his consciousness, shocking him. He had been content to be a loner. Now he rolled over in bed and touched the space where Amy lay earlier. He wanted to talk to her. Talk.

The realization stung him. General conversation was a waste of time. Yet, he wanted to shoot the breeze with Amy, find out how she was feeling, and ask if Bobby was all right.

He was losing his blanking mind. He sat up and grunted. Why, after spending his whole life learning to hide his feelings, did he want to share them with Amy, a woman with her troubling baggage and a sickly kid?

Until now, with determined strength, he'd built a life with no commitments. An existence easy to control, managed by the fact that he was never in one place for long and didn't date any woman long enough to get seriously involved in her life or her problems.

Wes had asked him and now he wondered, "What makes Amy special?" Okay, she was pretty even with frizzy strawberry-blonde hair, but she wasn't an exceptional beauty.

Amy's spirit called to him, with her determination to make the farm pay and her watchful care of Bobby. Nothing phony about her either, only kindness and honesty, not to mention her pouting lips, ripe breasts, and slender thighs that had engulfed him. He shook off his thoughts and went to take a cool shower.

Dressed in blue jeans and a gray t-shirt, he pulled on his cowhide boots and wrote a note to let Amy know he'd be working out of town for some time.

With the miles separating them, he'd regain his equilibrium. He sure didn't have it now. He ignored the pang that shot through him when he realized he wouldn't be seeing her today.

He had to go back to his ordinary life. Handling a bucking bronco seemed easier than managing his confused emotions.

He'd drive to the stables outside of Sacramento, where his stallion was corralled. Spirit needed to be ridden as much as he needed the exercise.

With the sun overhead, the wind in his face, and a stead moving under him, he'd regain his self-control. It'd be good to be back in territory he understood, no wild feelings, no gut-retching decisions. He sucked in a quick breath and left for Sacramento.

# CHAPTER 23

**On** the morning of the pumpkin patch grand opening, Amy unlocked the door to the newly painted tack room, now the gift shop.

Would Wyatt show up? She stopped that thought. She didn't have time to think about anything but getting the pumpkin patch ready for the visitors.

Just then Vanna came up beside her, carrying a box and a shopping bag in her arms. She set her packages on one of the picnic tables. "Amy, the place looks great."

"Thanks. I painted the room and Wyatt put up the shelves and brought in the tables. I couldn't have done this without his help."

"Nice to have a hunk around the place." Vanna winked. "Anyway, I've got Laurie's crafts. She knitted the cutest hats for babies and kids. See, orange pumpkins and black cats with ears sticking up."

"They're wonderful." Amy turned one over and examined it. "I know they'll sell." She rummaged through the bag. "Whoa, I don't know how she finds the time to make so many."

"She and her mom and grandma make them so fast, they're a little factory." Vanna reached into the box. "Here's homemade candles and her husband made wooden blocks and these cute wooden cars."

"Man, these are great. I'll buy a candle and Bobby would love one of these cars."

"Hey, Amy, we're supposed to make money, not buy everything." Vanna laughed.

"You're right, but they're hard to resist." She grinned. "I hope the moms and kids feel the same way. We can tag them and put them on the shelves around the room. And I got paper decorations. I thought we could string them up in the windows and hang them from the rafters above the picnic tables." Amy held up a paper ghost. "Spooky."

They both laughed.

"I'm excited. This place looks better than I could've imagined—Vanna, what if nobody comes?"

"They will." Her friend arranged the kid's hats in piles.

"So much depends on this day being a success. I sure need the money and I know Laurie does too."

Well, the kids from my preschool class are coming. They're all excited. I had them meet at the school playground. I'll get them and bring them here in the van. Between word of mouth, and the ads and tweets, people will be here. Moms on the way from the ice cream parlor with the vanilla ice cream for the pie a la Mode. Also, she made raspberry ice for Bobby and anyone else who wants some."

"Vanna, you guys are the best."

"Stop worrying. It's all going to work out. Got to get the kids. Be back soon."

"Okay. See you."

Vanna ran out, the screen door slamming behind her.

Amy stared at Vanna. What would Amy do with all the apple and pumpkin pies if no one showed up?

She winced at the thought. And the crafts her friends were depending on selling, what about those?

Think positive. She had to think positively. That's what she always told Bobby to do. Today, she realized it wasn't as easy to do as it was to say.

The sound of Wyatt's pickup truck interrupted her thoughts. He'd come after all. Relieved, she let out a sigh. In the back of her mind, fear of abandonment had caused her to believe he would never return. He'd walk out of her life just as her mother had done.

*** 

Wyatt hopped out of the cab and turned to see his brother's red sports car pull into the driveway.

"Hey, I didn't expect to see you here," Wyatt said as his brother got out of the driver's side of the vehicle.

"Not going to miss the big event." Wes hesitated and held up his hands. "That's if my sorry ass is welcome here." He grinned but stayed close to his convertible. "I like pumpkin pie as much as the next guy."

"Come and get some." Wyatt pulled Wes close and slapped him on the back, then released him.

He wondered how Amy would react when she saw his brother. He knew she hadn't seen him since Wes called her a slut at the restaurant.

She didn't have siblings and might not understand that many times, throughout the years, siblings fought and then forgave each other. It was the way it worked, especially with brothers. They were linked for life. Any woman involved with him would have to put up with Wes and his ways or the relationship wouldn't work.

"Come on, Wes, I'll formally introduce you to Amy. And this time, show some of your cowboy charm to her. I've seen how nice you can be when you want to."

"In other words, smile and keep my mouth shut."

"Yeah, you got it right," Wyatt agreed.

The aroma of apple and pumpkin pie permeated the room as they entered the remodeled tack room. The din of mothers' and children's voices filled the large room. It looked as if Amy wouldn't have to worry about having too much pie left over if the families eating at the table were an example of what could be expected for the rest of the day.

People milled around the edge of the room admiring the handicrafts Amy and her friends had for sale. A wooden truck caught his eye. He ran his hand over the smooth wood. *He* ignored Wes's look of surprise. *Bobby would dig this.*

True to his word, his brother made a sign of zipping his mouth closed.

In the crowded room, Wyatt spied Amy standing behind the cash register taking money from a mom. The sound of the cash register rang as he approached.

She glanced at him, her strawberry blond hair in a ponytail tied with a big black bow. In a slim-fitting orange blouse, tight black jeans, and orange pumpkin earrings swinging from her ear lobes, Amy pushed up her glasses from the bridge of her nose and grinned at him. *Damn, she's cute.*

"Wyatt."

"Hey," he said. A warm glow sparked in him, sending a hunger for her to shoot through him.

Her expression suddenly turned grim and her eyes narrowed as she looked at Wes standing next to him.

"Amy." Wes nodded.

Her body stiffened and her lips tightened to a thin line.

"I thought we could make a fresh start." He hesitated. "Sometimes I can be an ass."

"I'll attest to that," Wyatt added.

"Yeah, you can," she said.

Wes grinned and held out his hand. "Peace?"

"Yeah—okay." She shook his hand.

"The pie smells awful good." Wes sniffed and looked toward the kitchen.

"Take a seat and I'll bring you some." She smiled for the first time.

Wyatt stared at a kid sitting alone at a picnic table. The only boy who wasn't eating pie.

"Bobby."

"Hi, Wyatt." Bobby scooted over, making room on his side of the table.

"Hey, big guy. This is my brother, Wes."

Wes sat across from them.

Amy came to the table and asked, "Do you want apple or pumpkin? Or a little of both?"

"Both sound good to me," Wyatt said.

"For me too." Wes grinned.

"Okay, I'll be right back."

"Not eating the pie, kid?"

"I have celiac disease. I can't eat it."

"Sorry." Wes cringed and seemed at a loss for what else to say.

"It's okay. Sophie made my special raspberry sherbet," Bobby said as if he was used to the awkward reaction.

Wyatt watched his brother squirm.

191

"Whoa, Bobby, I hope Sophie made enough sherbet for Wes and me too. Her sherbet is way too good to pass up."

Before he could answer, Amy was back with pieces of pie for them.

"Enjoy." She served the dessert. "I better get back to the cash register."

"Her son wiped a drip of the pink sherbet from his chin with the back of his hand. "The stuff's kinda messy. Mom says I gots to use my napkin, but I dropped it on the floor and now it's dirty."

"No worries, kid. I'll get you another one." Wes rushed from the table.

Wyatt sensed his brother's relief at being able to find an excuse to leave because he had never spent much time around kids, let alone a sick kid. Just then, Wyatt realized he didn't think of Bobby as sickly.

Bobby scooted closer and leaned against him. It seemed the natural thing to do, so he put his arm around the little boy.

"Mommy is busy. She can't find me a pumpkin til everyone goes home. But the best ones will be gone by then. There'll only be the ones nobody wants." The little guy stirred his sherbet and then licked the spoon. "Can you help me find a jack-o' lantern? Uh, after you eat your pie?"

Wyatt wanted to smile, but then he saw the little boy's serious expression and knew it was a huge deal.

"Sure, big guy. I'll eat in a hurry and we'll get out there and find a special one just for you."

"Wyatt?"

"Yeah."

"You can have some of my sherbet."

"Thanks." He gave the little boy a quick hug.

Bobby jumped up and ran toward the back of the room where Sophie was standing near a refrigerator.

Amy came back to the table with Bobby. She carried a bowl of sherbet. "Wyatt, Bobby wants you to have some of his sherbet."

"Thanks. Join us."

"I'd love to, but I'm the only one who runs the cash register. I used to be a bank teller, so my friends think I should do it." She flicked a stray hair from her face. "I hope you're liking the pie." She pushed her bangs out of her eyes. "We'll be closed at six. If you're still here, I'll make you dinner."

"I look forward to it. Let me know if I can help."

"Thanks—I will."

He watched the sway of her backside in the tight black jeans and thought about stripping the jeans down her firm legs and then carrying her to bed, after Bobby was asleep, of course.

When they finished eating, he and Bobby ran to the pumpkin patch. Wes followed close behind. Wyatt watched Bobby touch each pumpkin to see if it might be the right one for his jack-o'-lantern.

His brother stood next to him and back a few feet from Bobby.

"I never thought I'd see a time when you'd take interest in somebody else's boy," Wes whispered. "He's a cute kid. I'll give you that. But who's the father?"

Wyatt shrugged. "It doesn't matter."

A surprised expression spread across his brother's face. "But Wyatt..."

"You wouldn't understand."

"You got that right."

193

They walked behind Bobby, dodging the other kids that ran searching for their "special" pumpkin. A sense of peace spiraled through him as the patch filled with the sounds of happy kids laughing. They would never know the loneliness and abandonment he had experienced, never feel the void careless parents created in their unwanted children.

After seeing the bitter relationship and the breakup of their parents, he and Wes had agreed to stay unattached, with no wife and no children.

Then he'd observed Amy's grandparents cope with the ups and downs of their marriage, the financial slumps, and the loss of loved ones. But still, they stayed together. Wes hadn't had that advantage, but Wyatt had seen what a relationship could be when the two people worked together as a team. Yeah, sometimes life was tough, but wouldn't it be even harder without a partner to get your back when things were bad?

As the pumpkin patch filled with kids and their families, Wyatt had to admit Amy had done a spectacular job advertising the event.

"Wyatt, look," Bobby shouted. "Here's my jack-o'-lantern. The bestest ever." The little boy hugged a pumpkin big enough for Bobby to sit on.

Wyatt strolled around the pumpkin. "Whoa, big guy, this *is* the best. But I think we're going to need your wagon to bring it to the house." He looked at his brother standing in the field, a bored expression on his tanned face.

"Bobby, my brother can wait here and guard the pumpkin while we go get the wagon." He slapped his brother on the back. "Right, Wes?"

The look of boredom on his brother's face turned to disbelief.

Wes opened his mouth to speak, but before he could, Wyatt said, "It'll do you good to be out in the sunshine with the kids." He laughed. "We'll be right back."

"You owe me."

"Yeah, yeah." Wyatt knew he was in for it. His brother would get his revenge. Still, Wyatt smiled.

"Big time, Wyatt. You owe me."

They left Wes surrounded by squealing kids, a look of apprehension spreading across his face, a lost doggie in a herd of children.

Bobby ran toward the house and his red wagon.

It took longer to find and empty the wagon than Wyatt thought it would. He hoped Wes had stayed with the pumpkin. If he left it and some other kid got the one Bobby had picked out, the little boy would be heartbroken. The realization that the boy's feelings were important to him struck hard like a punch to his mid-section and for a second he didn't move, instead, he took a long slow breath.

When they got back to the patch, Wyatt noticed his brother talking to a willowy blond with straight hair hanging down the back of her white shirt. Her shapely rear was expertly displayed in a short denim skirt. Black-tooled cowgirl boots hugged her slender calves.

"Vanna," Bobby called.

The woman turned and waved when she heard him. "Hi, Bobby."

Wyatt saw her amazing green eyes dance with pleasure when she returned her attention to his brother. Leave it to Wes to find the only single female in the whole field of mothers and their kids. Radar, that's what the guy had, able to zero in on anything hot.

"Wyatt," Vanna said.

"Hey."

"Teacher, did you see my pumpkin?" Bobby asked eagerly.

"Yeah, it's great. It's going to make a wonderful jack-o'-lantern." She bent down and gave him a quick hug and then released him.

"Wyatt, look at all the people. I'm so happy. It's busier than I could've imagined. And the maze looks great. Amy told me all the work you did on it."

"Johnny did the most of it." He watched Bobby wander a few feet away to talk to another kid then glanced back. "I see you've met my brother."

"Yeah. He was nice enough to volunteer to help me with the kids. Offered to get their pumpkins to my van. I was wondering how I was going to do it." She grinned openly at Wes.

"No kidding?" Wyatt gave his brother a "thumbs up." "Well, I know how he feels about the little kiddies." *And sexy blondes.*

He watched Wes's eyes follow the swell of Vanna's breasts through the opening of her shirt, unbuttoned, no doubt, while was she helping the children.

"Missed a button," Wyatt whispered to her.

Her cheeks colored to deep pink as she quickly buttoned the shirt.

He ignored the glare Wes sent him. Instead, he smiled at his brother. It wasn't returned.

They all walked back to the farmhouse.

Maybe he should warn Vanna what a womanizer Wes was. Nah. She'd been an actress living alone in Los Angeles. She could take care of herself. Even so, he could see the craving in her eyes when his brother smiled at her. Damn, that guy could, as the old saying went, "Charm the birds out of the trees," when he wanted to.

Amy joined them just as they reached the house. "We're closing up for the night."

"I better get the kids rounded up," Vanna said somewhat breathlessly. "I'm taking them back to the preschool. Their moms are picking them up there. I'll come back and help you clean up if you need me. Wes, do you want to drive along with me?"

"Whoa, you're a tall drink of water," a female voice said.

Wyatt spun around to see Nan, Amy's friend from San Francisco, standing behind him. Black knee-high boots gripped her long slim legs and jeans hugged her tight rear end. A form-fitting black sweater pressed her ample breast, pushing them up and molding them into inviting morsels begging to be touched.

"Hi, all." Her red lips curved up in a smile.

"Nan." Amy hugged her friend. "I didn't expect to see you today. Didn't think a kid's pumpkin patch would bring you up here."

"Can't let your big day go by without showing up," Nan cooed, but she didn't look at Amy, her eyes were still on Wes.

She moved closer to him. "Who are you?"

"I'm Wyatt's brother."

"Right." The corners of her mouth twisted slightly. "So, he does have a brother."

Wyatt glanced at Vanna as a flush brushed her cheeks and her grin disappeared.

"Amy, you've been holding out on me," Nan continued. "But I've found him now." She laughed.

"Well—" Amy glanced first at Vanna and then at Nan.

"We were just going into the house," Wyatt said. "Nan, join us."

"Where are you going, tall brother guy?" Nan winked at Wes.

"Honey, wherever you want to take me." He hooked his arm with Nan's.

Vanna cleared her throat, but Wes didn't seem to hear her.

"Got a good sports bar in town, brother? I sure could use a cool drink."

"I can find something to quench your thirst." Wes pulled Nan to him. "Catch you all later," he said as he walked away with Nan on his arm and without a backward glance toward Vanna.

"I—" Vanna's voice cracked. "Uh—got to get the kids."

Wyatt watched her run in the opposite direction from Wes and Nan.

"Wait," Amy called after her.

Vanna continued to run.

"Wyatt, I didn't know there was a sports bar in town."

"There isn't, but I'm sure my brother will find some kind of drink for her."

Amy gaped, a pained expression on her face.

"I don't know what to say to you. Wes is—Wes." He shrugged and watched his brother disappear behind the farmhouse and then heard an engine turnover.

"I've never seen Nan act like that. I'm blown away."

"My brother does that to some females. It might do him good to meet a woman like Nan. Someone who knows how to handle him." He hesitated. "Hope Vanna isn't upset. I could see her cheeks were red."

"I've seen Wes twice, and both times he's managed to hurt someone's feelings."

"Yeah. I never know what he's going to do," Wyatt grunted. "Let's get Bobby and I'll fix dinner. You must be exhausted. Bet you'd like to put your feet up."

"That sounds fantastic, but first I should find Vanna and help her now that Wes isn't going to."

"Okay. Bobby and I can hold down the fort."

"Thanks. I—uh. Well, thanks."

Amy ran after her friend.

"Come on Bobby, let's get your pumpkin to the house."

"Wyatt, can we put it on the front porch?"

"Sounds good to me."

He pulled the wagon, with the pumpkin precariously balanced in it. Bobby skipped beside it. The little boy looked up at him, an expression of trust and affection on his young face.

"This is the funest day ever." Bobby grabbed his hand.

Anger toward the boy's dad flared. Where was the jerk? Why wasn't he taking care of his responsibility? Hard to understand how a man could walk away from such an amazing kid. The boy deserved his father. But Wyatt wasn't that man. Never could be.

# CHAPTER 24

"**Vanna,** wait up," Amy yelled, but her friend didn't slow down. Amy lost sight of her for a moment and sprinted until she saw her talking to a couple of boys, each carrying small pumpkins.

"Hey." Amy stopped and caught her breath. "I came to help you and the kids get their pumpkins to the van."

"Thanks. Come on kids. If you can carry your pumpkin, do it, but if it's too heavy Miss Amy will carry it for you." Vanna winked at her.

"Thanks." Amy wrinkled her nose back at her friend. "Okay, but I can only carry one at a time. Does anyone need help?"

A pale-faced little girl with bouncy red curls and huge blue eyes slowly raised her hand. "I do."

Amy leaned down and smiled. "What's your name?"

"Holly."

"Hi. Where's your pumpkin?"

The little girl pointed and Amy couldn't help but laugh that the delicately built kid had picked an oversized pumpkin.

Maybe someday she'd have a strawberry-haired baby like Holly. *Whoa, where did that come from?*

The idea of having another baby sent a slice of pain to her chest. Even though she dearly wanted them, she wasn't going to have any more kids. She couldn't take the chance that she'd pass on celiac symptoms.

If she married again, which was unlikely, she understood there was a probability of celiac appearing again. She loved Bobby more than life itself, but she wouldn't put another child through what he'd already had to endure, weakness, nausea, vomiting, and constant vigilance concerning every bite of food he took. Not to mention, other physical ailments he might have to deal with later in his life. The thought chilled her.

"Teacher." Holly pulled her arm. "Help me."

Amy picked up the pumpkin, relieved to find it wasn't as heavy as it looked.

She and Vanna marched with the kids while they all sang "The Itsy-Bitsy Spider." When they reached the driveway, she was glad to set the pumpkin in Vanna's van.

"Okay kids, everybody in the car," Vanna called.

Amy marveled as all the kids eagerly climbed in and put on their seat belts without complaining.

"I know my keys are in here somewhere." Her friend stood outside the driver's side door and dug in her purse. "Ah, found them."

"Vanna, your blouse is undone again."

"No." She quickly buttoned it. "I shouldn't have worn this old thing. But with the kids… Wyatt's brother probably thought I was coming on to him. I'm so completely embarrassed."

"I'm sorry about Nan. I've never seen her act like that. She should've seen Wes was with you."

"It doesn't matter."

Amy could see by her expression, it did matter. "Nan was wrong to do that."

Vanna shrugged. "When I lived in LA, I met a lot of good-looking jerks like Wes, who thought they were God's gift to women. They could turn their attention from one woman to another in the blink of an eye. I should be immune to guys like that by now." She flushed. "Nan probably saved me from making a fool of myself. I'm looking for more than Wyatt's brother has to offer. I came home for a new start and he's way too much like my past."

The melancholy tone in her voice belied the smile on Vanna's lips.

"The right guy is out there," Amy said.

"Tell him to hurry up. I'm not getting any younger." Vanna laughed, but a touch of bitterness sounded in her voice. "What about you and Wyatt? I noticed the way you looked at him when he couldn't see you. You love him."

"OMG, am I so obvious?" She glanced around the area hoping no one else heard what her friend said.

"Only to me. After all, I've known you since first grade."

"I've tried to be cool, but..." She sighed.

"I don't think he knows. If that's what worries you."

"It does. Damn, I know he's not interested in me. He doesn't want love and a family, but when I'm with him—how can I explain?"

"You don't have to."

"I want to. He's so good to Bobby and to me. It's just my imagination, but when we're all together, I feel like we're a real family. I never felt like that with my ex-husband, even though he's Bobby's father."

"And Wyatt?"

"Uh." Amy hesitated. "I'm not sure what he thinks of us," she whispered. "Maybe he doesn't have any thoughts about us at all."

"Why don't you ask him?"

"I couldn't do that. What if he doesn't care for us? What would I do then?"

"Teacher?" Holly said as she peeked out of the van window. "When are we leaving?"

Amy jumped and looked at Holly, wondering if she had heard the conversation.

"Soon," Vanna said. "Amy, your secret's safe with me. I'll never tell." She crossed her heart.

"Thanks."

Her friend glanced at the kids in the van. "I better go. Ciao."

Amy watched her climb into the driver's seat and slam the door. "See you."

She waved at her friend as the van backed out of the driveway.

***

In the farmhouse living room, Amy admired Wyatt, backlit by the flames in the fireplace. "Thanks for dinner. You and Bobby make a great omelet."

"Just call us anytime you need short-order cooks."

She chuckled, rubbed her arms, and glanced around the room for her sweater. "Man, it's chilly. Glad you made a fire. It's going to be a cold night. Autumn is definitely here."

He strode to the couch and sat down. A sense of desire rippled through her.

"Bobby didn't want the day to end." She set the baby monitor on the coffee table and, with a big sigh, sat on the couch, leaned back, and put her feet up on the wooden coffee table. "Wow, this feels so good."

"When you first told me your idea for the pumpkin patch, I wasn't sure it would work. You did a great job today."

"I was afraid I'd be left alone in the field of pumpkins with dozens of pies waiting to be served and no one wanting to eat them." She kicked off her shoes. "It looks like I'm going to have to get up early and make more pies before we open the pumpkin patch tomorrow."

She watched the flames in the fireplace. "Thanks to you and Johnny, the maze was a big hit, especially with the older kids. I couldn't have done it without you." She stretched content for the first time in months. "I couldn't have asked for a better day."

"Bobby said it was the "funest" day ever," Wyatt added.

"You helped make it fun." Their eyes caught and held. A shiver of longing danced in her core. Ignoring it she said, "I've never seen him so happy, yet so completely exhausted. He's going to sleep soundly tonight."

"You must be tired too."

"No. I feel strangely exhilarated."

"Adrenaline. Once it settles down, you'll relax and feel worn out. I know about that. I spend most of my time being thrown around by horses." He grinned. "Sometimes, after a hard day of landing on my rear, I feel that way. Even when I stay on the horse, which I do more often than not, adrenaline races in me for hours. My body aches with exhaustion, but I can't sleep."

"That must be awful."

"You get used to it. Even enjoy the sense of being completely alive."

"I feel alive when I'm with you." She didn't mean to say it, but the words came out before she could censor them.

His eyes widened, but he didn't speak. For a moment, the noise of the crackling fire was the only sound in the room. Then he gently pulled her to him and caressed her cheek. "Your skin is soft and you smell like pie and perfume." He took a deep breath. "Sweet and feminine."

He kissed her cheek and then the nape of her neck. She leaned against him and moaned with pleasure.

"Amy, come to bed with me."

"I thought you'd never ask." Breathless, she kissed him and took his arm. He grabbed the baby monitor and together they went out the back door toward the cottage.

**\*\*\***

Wyatt watched Amy roll over onto her back. Asleep, she purred quietly, her long strawberry hair spread out over the white pillowcase.

He studied her. Her natural beauty was displayed in the dawn's light. With the bed sheet at her waist, and pale pink breasts rising and falling with each breath she took, his need grew. She had to be exhausted from their night of making love, so he ignored his desire and let her sleep.

Unexpected thoughts churned in him and he worried. Something he'd never done until recently. Maybe because he'd lost his mother at an early age, for most of his life, he'd thought only of his wants and needs. Now concern for Amy and Bobby was foremost in his mind.

He agonized over Bobby's illness and Amy's lack of family support. He mulled over her deteriorating financial condition, even losing sleep because of the problem. What would happen if she tried to run the farm alone and failed?

He wished he could let her have the farm, let her putter in the garden, make pies, and work on her crafts. The responsibility of being the executor of Granny's will was also troubling him. If that wasn't enough, he wanted Amy. However, did he want a lifetime of responsibility for her and her son?

# CHAPTER 25

**Amy** sat at Granny's desk in the den and watched the rain come down. "I'm glad this rain came after the pumpkin patch closed."

Dressed in a pair of old blue jeans and a long blue cable knit sweater, Vanna stretched and sat up on the overstuffed sofa. "Yeah, me too. Kids and mud. Yuck."

Amy frowned as she calculated the final numbers for the crafts and added them to the pumpkins and the apple pies that were sold.

Vanna sneezed and stood up from the sofa. "Damn, I'm coming down with an early cold. Do you have any tea? I could use a cup."

"Yeah. Help yourself. I've got English breakfast and peppermint tea."

"Peppermint's perfect."

"I'm almost finished with the books. Make a cup for me too, and I'll meet you in the kitchen."

"Done."

Amy zipped her pastel pink sweatshirt and went back to work. "Whoa. I can't believe it," she whispered. *We did better than I could've imagined.* With a sense of satisfaction, she wrote a check to each of her friends for their part of the profit.

With the checks in her hand, she jogged to the kitchen. "Wait until you see how much we made." She waved the checks.

"Nice." Vanna folded the check and put it in her purse. She handed Amy a cup of tea, then sat at the table.

"Hmm, love peppermint tea." Amy took a sip.

"Speaking of love, how long is Wyatt going to be gone?"

"Until Thanksgiving. He has to make a living, you know. It's only three weeks. It just seems like forever." Amy put a teaspoonful of sugar in the tea and stirred. "Bobby misses him too."

"I ran into Wes the other day. You won't believe who was hanging on his arm." Vanna poured another cup of tea and took a sip.

"Nan?"

"No. Charlene. Decked full out in red leather."

"No way."

"Way. And I could hear her call him sugar as they walked by." Vanna giggled.

"They deserve each other." Amy laughed too. "I don't see how two brothers can be so different."

"You love Wyatt."

It wasn't a question so she didn't answer. "Vanna, you'll find someone."

"In a town this small? Not enough people. Sometimes I think I should've stayed in LA." She shrugged. "I was miserable in LA, too many people." She smiled. "Too small, too big, you see, I'm hard to please."

"You're not."

"Yeah, I am. Uh, someone did ask me out."

"Who?"

"Doesn't matter. Can't go."

"Why? Don't you want to?"

"The funny thing is I do. But Mom wouldn't like it. She couldn't understand."

"Who is it?"

"Manuel Gordon," Vanna's voice softened, "Manny?"

"He and his crew harvested Granny's apples and he's on the rodeo circuit with Wyatt. I didn't know you knew him."

"I kind of knew him in high school. We had a secret thing back then." Vanna blushed.

"You never told me."

"Never told anyone. I hadn't seen him since then. One day, he brought his sister's little boy to my preschool. When he came to pick up his nephew, we talked. Before I knew it, I was looking forward to seeing him whenever he came to school to get his sister's kid, Jesse. Manny is so easy to talk to."

"He seems nice. Gorgeous too. Tall, dark, handsome."

"Yeah, but—I." She sneezed three times and took a sip of tea and sneezed again.

"Vanna you're sick. You should be home in bed."

"You're right. I'm out of here."

"But what about Manny?"

"Like I said, I would if I could, but I can't. Mom would kill me."

"Why?"

Amy watched Vanna leave. She had the sense that her friend was relieved not to answer the question why Sophie didn't like Manuel and wouldn't want her to date him.

***

Nervous worry ran through Amy. Life was going well. Her history had shown that when she felt good, fate would move to ruin things.

The day after Bobby brought gluten-free food to school, the other kids stopped teasing him. Since then, he'd looked forward to going to school. She couldn't wait to tell Wyatt when he got back, after all the food was his idea. She knew just how to thank him. Her body warmed in anticipation.

After paying the monthly bills, she logged off her banking site. Money was tight, but if she was careful and there were no surprises, she and Bobby could make it until Christmas. In December she'd have a Christmas craft fair and sell Christmas trees and then money would start coming in again. She should relax, but after years of tension, she just didn't know how.

***

*Wyatt will be home soon.* Amy wanted everything to be perfect for him. With only one more day until Thanksgiving, she set the table in the dining room. She hadn't used the room since returning home, but it seemed the right thing to do for the holiday. She recalled his stories of Thanksgiving spent alone, while his mother worked at a restaurant. Wyatt was left with a frozen dinner, eaten in front of the TV.

She found Granny's best lace tablecloth, silver-plated utensils and Lenox dishes and placed them all on the old mahogany dining table. She'd bought orange candles for the table. Her hand shook as she placed the last candle in the crystal holder.

Risky to put too much importance on this dinner, she took a deep breath to calm down. It was only one meal in a year of nightly dinners. Right?

Yesterday the rain had pounded the old farmhouse. The TV weatherman had promised wet weather for at least another day. But even the storm couldn't dampen her mood. With Wyatt, Vanna, Sophie, Bobby, and Johnny coming to dinner, she had a sense of family. After so much disappointment in her life, this holiday she'd be truly grateful.

***

Amy turned off the bedside lamp and sank into the deep folds of her feather bed. Thanksgiving would be perfect. She closed her eyes and with a sigh she was about to drift off to sleep when a loud gust of wind rattled the shutters of her bedroom window.

She blinked and looked out into the darkness and imagined making love with Wyatt. Her body quivered and heated, remembering his touch. With her eyes closed, she could almost feel his kiss. *Soon.*

What time was it? Before she could roll over and check the clock, a drop of water hit her in the face, followed quickly by another. "What the—" For a moment she didn't believe what was happening. Drips came one after another at increasing speed.

In the dark, she sat up and squinted to see the ceiling. "Shit." She jumped out of bed and pushed it to the other side of the room.

In her nightgown, she ran to the bathroom and grabbed an armful of towels. She returned and tossed them on the wet oak floor in her bedroom.

She shivered as she jogged to the kitchen to get the biggest pot she could find.

With the metal pot on the floor, she lined it up with the drops falling from the ceiling. "Of all the nights," she mumbled. Ping, ping the drops sounded as they landed in the metal pot.

"Mommy, what's wrong?" Bobby walked into the bedroom, rubbing his eyes. He blinked at the dim light she'd turned on.

"Nothing, everything's okay. Go back to bed." She walked him to his room. "Sweetie, go to sleep. It's late. I'm going to bed too." She tucked in the blankets and kissed his cheek.

"Okay." He yawned.

In her room, she wiped up the water that had splashed on the floor and checked to see if the drops were going into the large stewing pot. Ping, ping, it was music to sleep by as long as the pot doesn't overflow.

Her body ached with exhaustion, but the rain pounding on the roof kept her awake. She stifled a yawn and lay back against the pillow. "Damn." She knew the roof was old, but why did it have to leak tonight, when everything was going so well? Still, wasn't that the story of her life? As soon as she began to relax and feel secure… Where the hell could she find money to patch the roof?

*Dear God, please don't let it rain in Bobby's room.*

# CHAPTER 26

**The** aroma of baked turkey and fresh bread wafted from the farmhouse kitchen into the dining room. Amy sat next to Bobby at the Thanksgiving table. As the people took a place at the oak table and under the candles' glow, she gazed at them, Sophie, Vanna, and Johnny, her new family. Her glance stopped at the vacant chair at the head of the table.

Where was Wyatt? He'd promised to be there. Why hadn't he called? If there'd been an accident and he was hurt, she'd have heard by now.

When the hors d'oeuvres were eaten, everyone began to ask if the turkey was ready. She couldn't wait any longer. Dinner had to be served.

A traditional meal of roast turkey, mashed potatoes, gravy, cranberry sauce, green peas and sweet potatoes was set on the sideboard. Homemade pumpkin pie and hand-whipped cream and raspberry sherbet would be served for dessert. Bobby said grace. She carved the turkey and served large portions to all.

Conversation flowed easily and no one was shy about asking for seconds of turkey and gravy.

"I may not have to eat for a week," Vanna said after swallowing her last bite of pie. "Here's to the chef."

"Best darned pie I've ever had." Johnny rubbed his stomach. "Can't decide if I like your apple or your pumpkin best."

"You can like them both best," Bobby said, a serious expression on his round face.

"A wise statement." Johnny grinned. "Yep, Bobby's got the right idea."

Everyone raised their glasses. "To Amy," they said in unison.

"To Mommy." Her son held up his glass of milk.

"To my family." Despite her disappointment at Wyatt not showing up, she smiled.

"Here, here," they shouted.

"Mommy, can I have more sherbet?" Bobby asked.

Everyone roared with laughter.

"You sure can."

"If you could make apple pie ice cream, Amy, you'd make a fortune." Johnny dug into his last bite of dessert.

"Why I bet I could make the ice cream," Sophie said, her eyes sparkling.

"I just know you could," Johnny agreed.

***

Later, at the front door, Johnny offered to give Sophie a ride home." We can talk about apple ice cream." He laughed.

"Well, if it's all right with Vanna, I don't mind."

"Mom, I want to stay and give Amy a hand. You might as well go with Johnny."

Amy winked at Vanna and then gave Johnny and Sophie a hug. "Thanks for making the day so special."

"Thank you," they said in unison. She watched them get into Johnny's GMC pick-up truck and drive away.

When the door closed, Vanna said, "You know, after my dad was killed, my mom never showed any interest in men. But did you see the way she looked at Johnny at dinner tonight?"

"She stared at him all through the meal," Amy said.

"Yeah, and Johnny didn't seem to mind."

"No, not at all, and he's a heck of a nice guy."

"Is he? I'd hate to have my mother get hurt."

"Your mom could do a lot worse than Johnny."

In the kitchen, Amy surveyed the mess. "This is one time I wish I had a dishwasher."

"That's me." Vanna laughed. "You bring everything from the dining room. I'll wash. You can dry."

"Sounds like a plan. Thanks for staying."

"No problem. How else could I get Mom to need a ride?"

They both laughed.

Amy put on an apron. "It's good for Bobby to feel he has a family."

"You and Bobby will always be part of our family."

"I know and it means a lot."

An hour later, Vanna folded the dishcloth and rinsed the sink. "Too bad Wyatt couldn't make it. His not being here was the elephant in the room no one was talking about. They didn't dare look at the empty place—except Bobby."

"I'm glad no one asked where Wyatt was. It's so disappointing. I—"

"Oh, Amy."

"It's okay. I'm just upset because he let Bobby down. I saw him with a sad expression in his eyes. I shouldn't have allowed him to get so close to Wyatt. He was starting to think of him as his daddy."

"Kids are resilient," Vanna said as they walked to the front door. "I work with them every day. He'll be fine. And Wyatt may have a good excuse."

"It's better he's not here. I wouldn't be in the mood to listen to his pathetic excuses. I'd have a few choice words for him. He hurt Bobby's feelings and that's not right." She shrugged. "Well, we didn't need him. We had fun anyway. He's the one who missed out."

"Right. It's his loss."

A gust of wind and rain hit them when Amy opened the front door.

"Whoa, I didn't know it was so stormy. Drive carefully."

"Yes, Mommy." Vanna joked.

Amy grinned, shut the door and leaned on it. Not wanting to ruin the dinner for everyone, she'd put up a good front tonight. Still, her heart ached and anger toward Wyatt burned in her.

She had believed in him and would have bet the world that he'd be there. She took a deep breath and pushed back the memory of the many times her ex-husband had failed to show up for important occasions. Why did she expect Wyatt to be any different? Weren't all men like that? Or was she just stupid enough to fall for the charming liars?

**\*\*\***

Amy carried Bobby from the couch, where he had fallen asleep, to his room. When she tucked him in, he woke up and asked her to read a book.

"Just for five minutes. Mommy, please."

Even though her feet were killing her and all she wanted to do was stretch out on her bed, she couldn't say no. "Okay. Five minutes. What do you want to read?"

"I want my new dog book." He grabbed it and then scooted over so she could sit on the bed with him.

"Wyatt says some dogs are real good on the farm. He marked them. See? He knows lots of stuff about farms." Her son's eyes twinkled with excitement as he spoke.

Bobby had spent the day waiting for Wyatt. Anger toward him flared. Even if he didn't want to see her, at least he could've called.

With the book open on the page of border collies, she read about the animal considered to be the smartest breed. The dog did seem to fit the bill, friendly, good with kids, and easy to train.

"Wyatt says lots of kids get puppies at Christmas time. But if you gets one at Christmas, you gots to be sure the puppy doesn't eat stuff off the tree. Cause they're not good for dogs. And..."

"Slow down.

"But Mommy, you said I could get a puppy. And Wyatt says."

"I don't care what he says," she said too loudly.

Her son frowned and a confused expression spread across his young face.

217

"Uh—I just mean it's been more than five minutes. You better go to sleep." She forced a smile. "Sweet dreams."

He looked as if he was about to ask a question, but instead, he said, "Night."

He seemed smaller than usual, sleeping in his bed and holding his favorite Teddy bear.

She shouldn't take her annoyance out on Bobby. He deserved better. Tonight, she realized how important Wyatt had become to him and how much Bobby believed in the man's opinions. He was a role model, a father figure. How could she tell him Wyatt didn't want to be in their family?

She quietly closed the bedroom door.

"Damn you, Wyatt."

***

The wind kicked up, pounded the house, and rattled the upstairs windows. Amy lay in her bed and listened to nature's rage. Lights flashed in the dark sky and thunder exploded sounding like cannon fire.

She sat up in bed and willed herself not to be afraid. Was Bobby scared?

On tiptoe, she walked to his bedroom and peeked in. Unperturbed, he slept.

With a sigh of relief, she sprinted to her bedroom. The pot catching the rainwater was just about to overflow. She quickly emptied it into the bathtub and then returned to the bedroom.

Another clap of thunder shook the walls. With a look toward heaven, she whispered, "Remember don't let it rain in Bobby's room, please."

Wearing her pink flannel nightgown and fuzzy pink slippers, Amy made no sound as she went to the kitchen for another pot to catch the drips coming faster from the ceiling in her room.

She was searching for a larger one when the pans tumbled from the cupboard making a loud clatter. "Shit," she swore under her breath and hoped Bobby didn't wake up.

# CHAPTER 27

**Wyatt** squinted in the dark to see past the windshield wipers pushing the torrent of rain aside. There it was, Granny's old farmhouse, drenched but welcoming.

He drove the pick-up truck into the driveway and turned off the engine. Guilt raked him. He should have called Amy today. Somehow, he couldn't bring himself to do it or to sit through Thanksgiving dinner pretending everything was fine.

Not until he talked to Amy in private and straightened things out between them. Then he could relax.

Why was the holiday a big deal anyway? It had been just another work day for his mother, a waitress. As a kid, he never paid attention to the day. After his mom's death, there didn't seem to be a reason to celebrate.

But to Amy it was major. She'd called it the second most important holiday of the year, with only Christmas more significant. *Hell.* He should have phoned her before dinner.

He jumped out of the truck. Pain shot down his back. Yesterday he'd been thrown from a horse, his fault for not keeping his mind focused on his day job.

With a grimace, he limped toward the house, his head down against the stinging rain.

At the front door, he stomped the water from his boots, and cringed as pain radiated up his back. He shook the raindrops from his hair and punched the doorbell.

About to ring the bell again, the door flew open. Amy stood guarding the entrance. Her strawberry blonde hair lay over her shoulders, messy, curly, sexy, just the way he liked it. The nightgown she wore hugged her curves and accented her breasts, making his hands tingle with the desire to caress them. But fire flared in her eyes and anger warned him not to touch her.

It wasn't going to be easy telling her the things she needed to know. He took a deep breath. "It's kind of wet out here. You going to let me in?" He smiled.

She stood her ground at the door. "It's late."

Just then lightning lit the sky and thunder boomed.

"We have to talk." He pushed past her, twisting his back as he did. He sucked in a groan.

"What's wrong? What's happened to you?" She quickly shut the door behind them.

"Nothing. It's just a back spasm. I'm getting too old to keep being thrown off a horse." He chuckled without humor and entered the living room.

"You're only twenty-nine."

"Thirty in December. I started when I was sixteen. That's a lot of years for any man to be bucked off a horse."

He put his arm around her, pulled her to him and breathed in her vanilla-scented perfume. "You're beautiful and you smell good too."

"Don't." She pulled away. "Have you been drinking?"

"No—look, I should've been here today. I had a decision to make. I didn't feel I could come to the house again until I'd made it."

She stared at him, anger blazing in her eyes. "Bobby waited for you."

He looked away. Had she been waiting too? He exhaled loudly. "Whatever I tell you now, I care about you."

"What are you saying?"

"As executor of Granny's will, I'm charged with doing what she wants. It might not be what you need. But I have to execute Granny's wishes as stated to me verbally and in her will."

"I don't get it?" She crossed her arms.

"My back is killing me. I need to sit down?"

"Sit."

He sat stiffly in a straight-back chair near the fireplace. "Amy, I admit the apple sale and pumpkin patch went better than I thought it would. But it can't sustain you and Bobby. It doesn't guarantee your future." He adjusted his position hoping to find relief from the backache.

"To run the farm successfully, this place needs new irrigation equipment and young trees for the orchards to replace an aging stand. The barn is rundown and will need remodeling to accommodate new equipment. The Christmas trees need reseeding." He took a breath.

Her eyes narrowed and her mouth tightened.

When she didn't speak, he stood in front of the fireplace and wondered how to continue. He shivered. A hot cup of coffee would be welcome, but it didn't look like he was going to be offered anything, except the door.

"Amy, you were a kid when you first saw Granny's farmhouse and you still see it with the eyes of a child. But the roof is in bad shape. I wonder if it will last another winter. Not only that, I checked the basement and there were signs of termites. Some of the wooden studs and flooring will need to be replaced soon. I haven't checked everything out, but it stands to reason the years without maintenance have damaged the place."

"What are you trying to say?"

"I should have told you all this at the courthouse on the first day. But you were so sad, so vulnerable—I just couldn't add to your grief. By not telling you the problems in detail, I gave you false hope. That was a mistake. I realize that now."

"Why are you bringing this up?"

He ran his hand over the stubble on his chin. "Before Granny died, she put out feelers, hoping for a quick sale of the farm."

"What?"

"Yesterday a real estate agent sent me an offer for the farm, house and land. It's an excellent offer considering today's economy and the condition of the land and buildings."

"I don't believe it." She shook her head. "The farm has been for sale the whole time I've been here and you didn't think to tell me? I knew you had realtors look at it, but you never said it was actually on the market."

He watched her push a wayward strand of hair back from her face and stare at him. Anger flashed again in her hazel eyes.

Only the sound of the rain, pounding on the roof, interrupted the lengthening silence.

Finally, she said, "Why did they send the offer to you? I'm Granny's granddaughter. It should've come to me."

"I'm the executor." *As well as half-owner.* He moved away from the fireplace. "It's a good offer. An agricultural conglomerate wants the land. They have a processing plant in Sacramento and Granny's property is in the perfect spot for one of their farms. In this market, I didn't expect the farm to sell, not with a flood of new properties coming up for sale every week.

"This is an organic farm. Always has been. Is the conglomerate organic?"

"Uh—no."

"So, they'll spray pesticide, destroy our orchards and plant non-organic trees.

He hesitated, not wanting to anger her more.

"They don't produce organic, but will they fix and use the house and barn?" she asked.

"To make it worth their while, the house and all the outbuildings, including the cottage, will have to be knocked down to make room for more apple orchards."

She gasped.

"It's a tradeoff to make your future financially stable. With the money from the sale, you could take care of Bobby's medical needs without worrying about how to pay for the insurance and doctors. Even with the outrageous real estate prices in San

Francisco, you might have enough for a down payment on a small condo or you could buy in Sacramento if you wanted to."

She glared at him, an expression of disbelief on her pretty face. Then, as if he'd knocked the breath out of her, she slumped onto the sofa and put her hands to her face. He thought he heard a sob, but with the storm, he couldn't be sure if it was her or the wind.

The information seemed to deflate her. The determined spark of life he'd seen and admired in her since she arrived, was gone.

He grunted. The day in the pumpkin patch, he'd noticed joy in her expression and the memory sent a pang of guilt running through him.

"Hell. Amy, I didn't want the position of executor for Granny's will. She asked and I said I would. I'm just a damned cowboy. I don't want to run people's lives. That's never been my goal." He stopped and took a slow breath. "I don't break promises. Yesterday, I called Judge Wilcox. He told me to follow the dictates and the spirit of the law and do whatever Granny wanted. How I feel has nothing to do with what I'm doing now. It's my job as executor."

"Even if I don't want to sell?"

"Granny wanted the place on the market. She was clear about that. Your grandmother said she knew you better than anyone else in the world. As a kid all you talked about was living in the city. Not a life on the farm. She understood the heartbreak and struggle farming brings." He moved closer to her and she shrank from him.

"Amy, Granny loved you and thought this was best." Wyatt spit out stale air. His argument had come full circle.

"Why did you let me think I could stay here? Why help me build the maze? You could have told me about the sale when I opened the pumpkin patch—or when I was in your bed," she hissed. "Why not tell me then?"

Before he could answer, she continued, "You tricked Granny, an old woman who needed your help and got her to sign half the property over to you. Now you want your money out of the deal."

She trembled. "You've waited long enough and now you want your profit. You're a money-grubbing, uh—I can't think of a word bad enough to describe you." She gasped. "Bobby. How can I tell him? What will I say? He loves you and the farm." Her hand flew to her mouth.

He reached for her. "Amy, try to understand what…"

"Stop." She yanked her hand from his. "I don't want to hear anymore. I feel sick when I think I let you touch me. Sicker when I think about how losing the farm is going to rip Bobby apart. He thinks it belongs to him. He won't understand. He's already been betrayed by his father and now you've betrayed him."

"That's not fair. You know I care about Bobby. The money is for him. It gives him a chance for financial security."

"All you care about is money. That's all you talk about. There's more to life than cash. How about the love of family or peace of mind? Or doing something important for your community? Or—" Her eyes blazed. "There must be a way to reach you. Wyatt, don't you understand? I can pass on the tradition of family farming and good values to Bobby. Something on this earth will belong to him, be his alone."

At that moment, he realized he loved her, and knew he always would. But a glance at her expression told him she'd never believe him if he told her now.

"Wyatt, you piss me off. You hold riches way too close, so close you can't see the value of anything else." She glared at him. "Why don't you answer?"

"How's Bobby going to get along without cash?" He slammed his hand on the coffee table. "How is he going to get the medical care he needs?"

She opened her mouth to speak but closed it again.

"If you want to talk about peace of mind, how about medical insurance for Bobby and a savings account for his college? That would give you big-time peace of mind." He held out his hands and rubbed his fingers together. "Money, a broken-down farm needs it, whether you want to admit it or not."

He paced in front of the fireplace. "There's no happiness when you can't pay the bills. I sure know that. I grew up hand to mouth, never knowing where I was going to sleep or if I'd have dinner at night. I think you'd want more than that for your son. I shouldn't have to tell you he needs financial security."

"Stop." She held up her hand. "No more. I can't stand to hear anymore. Just leave."

"I'll send you the offer. You can look it over."

"Do whatever you want. I'll never sign the papers. You can't make me." She got up and walked to the front door. "Go. And remember I still own half of this place. If I have to get a second job to buy you

227

out, I will. Now get out of my sight. I never want to see you again!"

Her words hit like a punch to his gut. He reached for her hand. "Amy, don't say something you'll regret. This isn't about us and how we feel about each other. You have to understand that. Don't confuse the issue. I still—"

She yanked out of his grasp. "Get the hell out of *my* house."

He hesitated. But seeing her rage, he walked out the front door, slamming it behind him.

# CHAPTER 28

**Amy** jumped when the front door banged shut with such power the windows of the old farmhouse rattled. She thought they might shatter. They didn't, but without Wyatt, she'd never put her heart back together.

"Damn him."

Upstairs, she couldn't sleep. The memory of Wyatt's gentle touch and demanding kiss taunted her. She yearned for the feel of him pressing against her, holding her, and taking her to heights she'd never before experienced. Tormented, she stared into the darkness.

***

Early Friday morning, the rain finally stopped and the sun returned.

Did Wyatt sleep on the farm last night? Amy pulled the lace curtain back from the bedroom window and looked out to the cottage.

If she were honest, she'd admit wanting him even now. Since the time she saw his smiling face that first day in high school, she had been attracted to him. Even then, she'd been warned away from him by her grandmother. "Wyatt is a wild kid. The town's folk say he'll come to no good. I hope they're wrong, but stay away from him," Granny had said.

If Amy had listened, she wouldn't be aching for his touch, desiring to be held in his arms and longing to be told he loved her. *You're a fool.*

A door opened and Wyatt, in a navy business suit and wearing a white dress shirt and a blue tie, stood on the cottage porch. She'd never seen him dressed in anything but casual shirts and jeans. He radiated power and was devastatingly handsome, the jerk.

He tossed a huge duffel bag in the back of his truck and drove away. Where was he going? Was he moving out? Or was he meeting with the realtor, to sell the farm? Could she stop him?

The dream of a relationship with him was over. She moaned. What she needed now was a job to help her get money to keep the farm running and buy Wyatt out. It would take years to pay him, but if she could convince him to let her make payments… There had to be someplace in town that needed part-time help.

She hadn't worn her gray wool suit with its two-button jacket and pencil slim skirt since she lost her job at the bank. Her black leather pumps still fit, though they weren't as comfortable as she remembered.

She blinked to moisten her contact lens and then brushed her hair and twisted it into a tight bun at the back of her neck. She glanced in the mirror that hung over the dresser. A serious-looking businesswoman stared back at her. Would it be enough to convince someone to give her a job?

Downstairs in the kitchen, she saw Bobby sitting at the table. "Finish breakfast, big guy. You'll be late for school."

"It's Thanksgiving vacation. I don't have school." He smiled his mouth full of scrambled eggs.

She resisted telling him not to talk with his mouth full. "Honey, you're going to stay at Vanna's school for a few hours today. Okay?"

"It's fun."

At the daycare center, she kissed his cheek and watched as he happily ran to the school's front door. He stopped and threw her a kiss before he entered the building. Her heart squeezed. She'd do whatever was necessary to keep the farm for him.

A headache pounded over her right eye. She had walked the main street and talked to every store owner in town. Hope there might be a job faded. The owners all said the same thing, "With the closing of the mill, business is slow. We just don't need any help right now." Though people were nice and promised to let her know if anything opened up, she saw in their eyes they wouldn't call. Disappointed, she'd entered the Volvo and sat and stared out the windshield to the main street. She'd been sure there'd be something for her.

With a deep breath to calm her nerves, she drove into a parking space in the grocery store parking lot. If Mike, as manager of the store, didn't give her a job, she was lost.

She smoothed her skirt, tucked a stray hair back into her bun, and entered the building.

He hadn't spoken to her since their disastrous night out. She'd probably be the last person he'd want to see. But as the manager of the biggest retail outlet in town, he was more likely to have a position.

Heat flushed her cheeks when she thought of the night at the restaurant when Wes had called her a slut in front of everyone, much to Mike's shock.

She couldn't blame him for not dating her again. And that night sure didn't help her social standing in Sierra Creek. He could have taken the view that it was Wes who was in the wrong, but he hadn't. Oh well, all she needed from him was a job. He didn't even have to talk to her while she was working if he didn't want to.

A middle-aged woman at the first cashier's stand smiled.

Amy grinned back. "Hi. I was wondering if there are any job openings at the store."

The woman thought for a moment, her forehead wrinkling as she did. "Nothing full-time, but we got a couple of part-time positions."

"That's perfect. Is Mike here today?"

"Let me check for you, honey."

The woman pressed the button on the intercom and called the office. "There's a lady here who wants to see Mike."

"What's her name?"

Amy heard Mike's voice.

"Amy Long," Amy said loudly, so he could hear her.

"Ask what she wants," he said gruffly.

"Here honey, why don't you talk to him?" The woman allowed Amy to speak into the microphone.

"Hi Mike, it's Amy. I thought I could talk to you for just a moment."

"The store is busy. I don't have time for this."

She glanced around and saw the store seemed unusually quiet, but she didn't contradict him. He might be hectic in the office even though the store seemed slow. "I hope I'm not bothering you."

"Cut to the chase, Amy. I don't have all day."

The woman in the check stand, cringed but didn't speak.

Amy flushed, then reminded herself any embarrassment was worth it if she could get a job and be able to buy the farm.

"I'm looking for a job. I've got experience in retail and as a cashier and even a few hours of work would be fine."

There was just the slightest hesitation and then he said, "Got nothing. No openings right now. You can go online and fill out an application if you want. But I wouldn't expect there'd be anything in this part of California."

The intercom went dead.

Mike wouldn't give her a chance, didn't want her around, and even lied to her, not realizing she knew about the two job openings in the store. He wasn't even polite enough to end the call by saying "Goodbye."

Tears of frustration burned in her eyes. "Thanks for your help," she whispered to the woman cashier and then rushed to the exit.

In the Volvo, she let out a cry. The farm was going to sell. She couldn't stop it.

At Christmas, she'd planned to have a big tree with all the trimming and was going to surprise Bobby with a Border collie puppy, the perfect dog for a farm. Now they probably wouldn't be living there. She wiped a tear from her cheek.

"Oh God, if we can't keep the farm, where will we go? What will I do?" Where would she and Bobby spend Christmas?

# CHAPTER 29

"**Wyatt**, are you sure you want to do this?" Judge Wilcox asked. "It is not necessary."

Wyatt brought his attention from the view of Sierra Creek's main street to focus on the middle-aged judge sitting behind a mission-style desk in the book-lined office.

"Yeah. I've spent the last three weeks thinking about it." He caught the eye of the man and noticed the tentative expression. "I know what I'm doing. Christmas will be here in a few weeks and I want this over with by then."

"All right, but you're going against Granny's wishes. She wanted you to sell, not do this."

Wyatt grunted. He hated explaining his motives, but the judge had to understand. "She wanted Amy to be happy. I'm helping Granny make that come true."

He cleared his throat. "You know my dad deserted me and my mom when I was a kid."

"Yes."

"I never told you, but after my mom died, Amy's grandmother helped me. She never talked to anyone or made a big deal about it. Just gave me support when I needed it. Made sure I had a place to live and enough to eat. And she taught me good values. Something money can't buy." He paused and ran his

Reggi Allder

hands through his hair. "I owe her a debt that's hard to repay. Money won't do it, but maybe this will help balance my liability and give another kid a chance."

He watched the judge's features tighten as his eyes narrowed. "I see."

"This is a way of paying Granny back."

The older man glanced at his watch. "It's early. I'll have the papers ready by the end of the day. Come back then."

"Thanks, Judge Wilcox."

***

Almost cold enough to snow, it was beginning to feel like Christmas. Usually her favorite time of year, Amy fought the despair that threatened to overwhelm her. For Bobby's sake, she had to be outwardly optimistic even if she didn't feel it.

In the early morning air, she shivered and quickly entered the farm's craft shop. The sales of the handmade ornaments, tablecloths and Christmas trees had exceeded her expectations. If only the shop could have another busy day.

She took off her wool coat and hung it on a hook near the door and adjusted the collar of her red turtle neck sweater. From the pocket of her blue jeans, she pulled out the list of things to be done today and scanned it. Yesterday she'd sold the last tree topper. Her friend, Laurie, would bring in more today.

Amy turned on the lights and strings of white twinkled from the rafters. The ornaments her friends had made sparkled on the huge Christmas tree in the corner of the room, all of them for sale. The neon sign in the window read, "Open."

"Hi, Amy." Johnny popped his head in the front door. "I'm going up to the Christmas tree grove to chop down a few more trees. I'll bring them back and set them up."

"Thanks, Johnny. Did you have breakfast?"

"Yep, no need to feed me this morning." He winked.

Not a guy to waste words. The man was gone before she could say anything else. He'd taken on the job of cutting Christmas trees and bringing them to stand next to the shop so people could choose one.

For those hardy families who wanted to cut their own trees, he took them out and made sure everyone returned safe and sound with a tree in hand.

Even though all seemed to be going well, happiness eluded her. No matter how much money she made with the crafts and tree sales, it wouldn't be enough to buy out Wyatt.

The battle to keep the farm was lost. It was just a matter of time until she had to move. She prayed Bobby could at least spend Christmas there.

"Amy, where do you want the rest of these little Christmas Bears?"

She looked up to see Vanna enter the shop carrying a cardboard box, her nose red from the cold weather.

"I guess we could put them on the shelves next to the reindeer."

"Okay. Whoa, looks great in here. Very festive." Vanna tossed her coat on a hook next to Amy's. "Should I start the Christmas music or will you go nuts if you hear another carol?"

"Put it on." Amy laughed. "I can take it."

She helped Vanna fill the shelf with Christmas bears.

"Have you heard from the realtor?"

"No, and it's been days and days. Wyatt said he'd send paperwork so I could see the offer, but I haven't received anything. It's pretty annoying. I'm just hanging here on pins and needles."

"Maybe the people who made the offer changed their minds."

"Could be," she said but didn't believe it.

"Call Wyatt."

"That'll be a cold day in…" She paused. "I don't know what to think. Bobby still talks about a puppy for Christmas." She sighed.

"I told Bobby we couldn't get a dog this year, but I can see by his expression he still hopes. He thinks I want to surprise him when I bring out a puppy on Christmas morning. I didn't have the heart to tell him we will have to leave the farm. He loves it here." She swallowed hard. "I can't break his heart—at least not until after Christmas."

"Amy." Vanna hugged her.

"Bobby hasn't asked where Wyatt is. I don't know what I'd say if he did. He must wonder why Wyatt stopped coming by. It's almost as if Bobby knows he shouldn't talk about it."

"Mommy." Bobby stood in the doorway still dressed in his pajamas. "My tummy hurts."

"Oh, honey."

She ran to him and when she lifted him, he cried.

"It hurts. It hurts." Tears ran down his face.

"Did you eat something that's not on your list?"

"No. Honest—I didn't."

"Are you sure?"

Bobby was crying too hard to answer.

"Vanna, I'm taking him to the hospital."

"I'll drive. Amy, you hold him."

\*\*\*

In an admitting office near the emergency room of Sierra Creek General Hospital, Amy paced. Vanna had gone with Bobby while she gave information to a clerk.

"How long before I can go to see my son?"

From her desk, a thirty-something woman frowned. "Mrs. Long, the doctor is taking good care of him. You can join your son as soon as you give me the needed information." She paused. "Now how are you going to pay for this visit?"

"What?"

"How are you planning to pay for the emergency room visit?" The woman asked. "Insurance, credit card, cash? We don't take checks."

"Well, I—it depends on how much it costs." Amy blinked and tried to focus. "Look, can't we do this later? I have to go to my son. He needs me." Her heart raced.

"I understand. Did you fill out the form? It's important we have that."

Amy filled in as much as she could and handed the paperwork back to the woman.

"And your payment method?" the woman asked again.

"Uh—credit card."

"Good. That should do it." The woman made a copy of the credit card and handed it back to her. "Thank you, Mrs. Long. You may go now."

She grabbed the card and ran toward the emergency room. *Dear God, please don't let the woman run the credit card and find out it's maxed out.*

What would the woman do if she knew the card was no good? Would the clerk have the hospital send

Bobby home without helping him? Could they do that?

"Excuse me?" she said to the first nurse she saw. "My little boy was just brought into the emergency room."

Before the woman could answer, Vanna ran up to her. "Come with me."

The nurse shrugged and walked away.

She followed her friend to a curtained cubicle.

"Bobby is in X-ray. He'll be right back."

"Oh good." She sat on a small stool next to the gurney in the enclosure.

Vanna paced. "The nurse asked so many questions about Bobby's medical history. I couldn't answer. I told them you'd be right back."

"Vanna, you're shaking."

"Am I? I was just so scared for Bobby."

"Me too." She glanced at her hands and noticed they were trembling. She took a slow breath and inhaled the antiseptic odor that floated in the room and listened to the foreign sounds of equipment in the emergency room.

"I'll call Laurie and see if she can run the craft shop today. I'll be right back. I don't think I'm supposed to use a cell phone in here."

"Oh. I hadn't even thought of that. The only thing I could think about was Bobby."

"It's all right." Vanna rushed out of the cubicle.

"Mommy."

Amy spun around to see Bobby sitting in a wheelchair his eyes teary. In the big chair, he seemed even smaller than usual.

A nurse helped her son onto the gurney and took the wheelchair away.

"Hi. Are you okay?"

"I—" Bobby stopped in the middle of the sentence and grimaced in pain.

She squeezed his hand. "Honey, it's going to be fine." She swallowed a sob and closed her eyes to hold back tears.

Just then a man walked into the cubicle. "I'm Dr. Johnson."

"Hello." She scanned the average-looking man with thinning hair and a kind expression on his face.

"The little guy tells me he's had a tummy ache for a day or so. He hoped it would go away as it usually does." He winked at her son. "This time, however, it doesn't look like celiac. After examining him, it's a different animal altogether. Still, we can't be absolutely sure until we get in there, but it's his appendix."

"No."

"Afraid so. You're right to be concerned. The main thing is to remove it. I've phoned the surgeon on call."

"Surgery?"

"As soon as possible."

"You mean today?"

"Within the hour, I should think."

She gasped. "He's so little." Blood drained to her extremities, pooling at her feet. She sat down on the stool. "Isn't there any other way?"

"No. More time has passed than I would have preferred. The longer we wait the better chance the appendix could burst, and then it would be dangerous for him."

"Oh."

"Does he have any allergy to medication?"

"Not that I know of."

"Good."

"When the other doc gets here, we're going to take that mean old appendix out, because you don't need it anymore. Right?" the doctor asked her son.

"Uh." Bobby's voice was no more than a squeak.

"Okay. Surgery will be over soon." Dr. Johnson walked away.

What would she do if anything happened to Bobby? She flinched and her heart thundered.

"Mommy?"

"Yes."

"I want Ted. He's under the front seat in the car."

"Well, I don't know if they allow…"

"Please." Bobby started to cry.

"Don't. I'll get your Teddy. If anyone asks, I'll just explain he's your favorite bear and you take him wherever you go." She kissed him on the forehead. "I'll be right back."

The stuffed animal was just where he said it would be. She grabbed the bear and rushed back to the emergency room.

***

A tall, slender woman with short brown hair, wearing aqua scrubs walked into the cubicle. "Mrs. Long?"

"Yes." Amy jumped up from the stool.

"I'm Dr. Susan James. I'll be doing Bobby's surgery, the appendectomy."

"Hi."

"Hey, Bobby, who's this guy?" Dr. James pointed to the stuffed bear.

"Ted."

"Hello, Ted." The doctor smiled. "I bet you'd like your bear to come with you."

Bobby nodded.

"Well, he's going to have to wear a mask. Everybody who goes to surgery has a special one, sort of like this." She pulled up a mask from around her neck and covered her mouth and nose, then took it off. "So, if you see me in surgery that's what I'll look like. I just happen to have an extra one for Ted. You'll get yours when you go into surgery. Okay?"

Bobby nodded again.

Amy smiled when the doctor put a disposal mask over the bear's face. "Thanks, Doctor."

"We're ready to go. Bobby, you can kiss your mom. You'll see her when you're done."

Amy gasped. "This is happening too fast."

"We'll take good care of him. The surgical waiting room is on the second floor. When the operation is complete, I'll see you there."

A nurse came into the cubicle carrying a clipboard. "Here's the consent form and a pen."

Amy signed the papers and said a silent prayer.

"Time to go." The nurse took the form and then pushed Bobby's gurney out of the cubicle.

Amy watched her son grip his teddy bear in a stranglehold, Bobby's eyes wide with terror.

# CHAPTER 30

**Thankful** she was the only one in the room, Amy collapsed onto the orange vinyl sofa in the small second-story waiting room and closed her eyes.

Was it possible she could lose Bobby and the farm at the same time? What did Granny say in her letter? Look for the bright side of life and you'll find it. *Granny, I've looked, but I can't do this alone. I need you.* She bit back a sob.

Futile adrenaline raced and her heart banged against her chest. Unable to sit any longer, she wandered around the room. How long did this kind of surgery take?

It seemed hours since she'd entered the waiting room. But without a watch or a cell phone, she couldn't be sure how much time had passed.

With her back to the door, she stared out the window to Sierra Creek, the town she'd hoped would be a haven. She moaned.

She'd lost Wyatt, even before she'd had a chance for a real relationship. "I can't lose Bobby too. Please not my baby," she whispered and wiped a tear from her cheek with the back of her hand.

When she glanced out the window again, the town looked peaceful, a picture postcard of the perfect small western town.

"Amy."

In disbelief, she turned and saw Wyatt standing in the doorway.

"I just heard about Bobby." He went to her and wrapped her in his arms.

She leaned against him, needing his strength, no matter their past disagreements.

"Don't cry." He gently wiped tears from her face. "Let's sit down." He led her to the sofa. "I got here as soon as I could. Have they told you anything yet?"

"No. How did you know?"

"Vanna called me."

Amy sat up and using her last bit of strength, pulled away from him. "I didn't expect to see you again. Thought you were gone for good."

Pain flashed in his eyes. "Amy, the last time I saw you I tried to tell you that I care."

"Do you? You could've fooled me."

"I'm not good at talking about my feeling." He hesitated. "I don't want to argue."

Only the sound of doctor's names being announced over the loudspeaker interrupted the quiet.

Wyatt stood, walked to the window and glanced out. "You mean more to me than I can put into words." He came to her and held out his hand.

"Don't." She turned to leave.

"Wait. You taught me it's not about money, not even about the farm." He paused and swallowed hard. "It's family. You and Bobby are my family."

Surprised, she gazed into his moisture-filled eyes.

She took his face in her hands, drew him close and kissed him firmly on the mouth, opening to let his tongue caress hers. She moaned and he deepened

245

the kiss. With her head resting on his chest, she listened to his steady heartbeat.

"Amy, Bobby is going to be all right. He has to be."

Without speaking, she clung to him.

The sun sank lower on the horizon and still, there was no word from the doctor.

"It's taking too long. Something must have gone wrong."

"We have to be patient." He pulled her back into his arms again.

"It's so hard to wait."

"I know." He caressed her cheek. "It's going to be all right—has to be."

Time passed slowly.

***

"Mrs. Long?"

Amy looked up to see Dr. James, still dressed in scrubs, enter the surgical waiting room.

"How's Bobby?"

"He's doing fine. The surgery went well."

"Thank God."

"The appendix was quite inflamed. It's a good thing he had surgery quickly. He's in recovery. When he's fully awake, they'll take him to pediatrics on the third floor."

"When can I see him?"

"It'll be a while before he's fully awake. You could wait in his room. The nurse will get the number for you. But first, why don't you and your friend get some coffee and a bite to eat in the cafeteria? There's enough time."

"Thank you. Thank you so much for taking such good care of my son."

"My pleasure, now don't worry. He only needs rest before he's back to himself." Dr. James smiled and then left the waiting room.

"Wyatt, he's going to be okay. I thought I might lose him."

For a second, he didn't speak, then he said, "Do you want to wait here or go get a snack?"

"I couldn't eat, couldn't hold it down." She paused. "I'm grateful you're with me."

"I wouldn't be anywhere else." Wyatt's blue eyes flashed. "I mean it."

He kissed her gently at first, and then with more fervor. He broke away and reached into his pocket. "I've been carrying this around. It's for you."

He opened a small maroon box. "I had it made from the stone we found at Cosumnes River the day we went on the picnic. We were right. It's a diamond."

The solitary jewel sparkled in the room's light as she turned the ring to view the small cut stone and the raised leaves carved on the gold band.

"The gold is from the California Mother Lode and the design has apple leaves carved on the side. A jeweler friend of mine and I designed it."

"It's magnificent." She held the ring to her heart.

"I've never said it to anyone, but Amy, I love you."

His words stunned her. She'd never imagined he'd feel that way about her.

"Will you marry me?"

"I— this is such a surprise. I need a minute to think."

"What would I do without you? Don't keep me waiting. The suspense is killing me."

"Yes," she said breathlessly. "Wyatt, I love you too—guess I always have."

He slipped the ring on the third finger of her left hand.

"The farm's not for sale. I've signed my half of the property over to Bobby."

"But I thought…"

"Amy, the only thing I want is your love."

## CHAPTER 31

Amy's heart raced. Christmas was on her doorstep and there was so much left to do. For the first time in years, there'd be a family Christmas dinner at the farm. She wanted it to be perfect. *No problems, please.*

Her son was home from the hospital and sales from her holiday fair were brisk. December hurried by, the days filled with work and making sure Bobby remained comfortable while he recovered from surgery.

Wyatt stayed home from the rodeo circuit, making it possible to care for Bobby and keep her Christmas business going at the same time

Love for Wyatt grew. Still, she'd worried she was rushing into the marriage ceremony. After all, only months had passed since she returned to Sierra Creek.

To maximize sales, the shop was open late. Wyatt attempted cooking a few dinners, from recipes he found online, to help out. She couldn't help smiling, remembering his pride when she had enjoyed the first meal he prepared.

"Thought I might have to feed the stuff to the horses," he'd said, and they'd burst into laughter. Soon, he'd go back to the circuit. She understood he had to. Still, she shuddered at the thought of being without him, even for a short time.

If she married Wyatt... If? Where did that come from?

After they took their vows, he'd be on the road going from town to city traversing the United States. Somehow, today the idea had more intensity, maybe because she'd become used to him at home as part of her family. She stopped. *Don't complain. Count your blessings, Wyatt loves you, Bobby is healthy and Christmas is coming.*

The TV weather station promised an especially cold winter. Amy crossed her fingers and hoped for a white Christmas. She zipped the blue down jacket Wyatt recently bought for her. Down was out of her budget, but he'd insisted. "Think of it as an early Christmas gift," he'd replied. He bought one for Bobby in army green, just what her son had asked for.

"When I'm at work, I want my family warm and cozy," Wyatt had declared. She'd hugged him and his responding kiss had sent a shiver of longing down her spine.

She closed the Christmas Shop and rushed to meet Wyatt and Bobby waiting in the pickup truck in the driveway.

In the passenger seat of the Ford F150, she smiled and gave Wyatt a quick kiss. He caressed her cheek with the back of his hand, and she held it, kissing the inside of his palm.

"Mommy, I'm wearing my red Santa hat. See?"

She twisted to glance at him. "Looks great—did you buckle up?"

"Yes, Mommy."

She snapped her belt closed and placed her hand on Wyatt's knee. "I'm so happy you're here to see the Sierra Creek tree lighting ceremony with us."

"I wouldn't miss it. Funny, it happens every year and I grew up in Sierra Creek, but never bothered to go, until now." He held her hand for a second then started the engine.

"They're going to light *our* tree," Bobby shouted. "Mommy gave it to the town. But I picked it out."

"Nice job, big guy." Wyatt glanced at Amy and winked.

"Bobby, you found the best tree ever," she assured him.

"As a kid, your mom had to choose a tree for the celebration. This year, it was your turn, Bobby."

"Maybe next time you can pick a tree, Daddy."

"Uh—thanks. I might."

They drove toward town singing Christmas Carols all the way.

The mayor and town council of Sierra Creek took the holidays seriously and every year tried to improve the decorations in town. The council had purchased new LED lights for the tree this year to save on the cost of electricity but decided to use the same vintage ornaments. That pleased her because she wanted Wyatt and Bobby to see the tree as she remembered it. The way Granny saw it before she died. Amy wiped her eyes.

"You okay, honey?" Wyatt slowed the truck and glanced at her.

"Yeah, just wondering what Granny would think knowing her precious tree would be in the town square again this year."

"Was it important to her?"

"Very."

"Okay, she'd be pleased."

She nodded and took a deep breath. "Yeah."

When they entered Main Street's downtown shopping area, they were greeted by a banner proclaiming, "Happy Holidays."

The council members encouraged merchants to participate in the celebration. Most shops put up lights and displays of some kind. This year, Sophie bought a miniature town with buildings, an ice-skating rink, people, and a snowman displayed in the window of her ice cream parlor.

Though it was early in the evening, the town sparkled in the dimness, a living holiday photo of the perfect small country town. She rolled down the window and the sounds of Christmas music wafted into the truck. People strolled on the sidewalk and occasionally stopped to enjoy the ornaments decorating the retail stores.

The town square, with its small park and bandstand, sat next to the city hall at the end of the street. Wyatt smiled as they drove through town. She recalled he and his mother didn't pay much attention to Thanksgiving or Christmas. He came because it was important to her.

"What are they going to do after they light the tree, Mommy?"

"Well, the high school band and choir are going to perform."

"And all the kids get a candy cane," Wyatt said.

"Can I have one?"

"Sure, Bobby."

"Growing up, my mom set up a little fake tree setup on the coffee table in our living room."

"Daddy, you didn't have a real one?"

"No, but we had candy canes. Every Christmas she bought a few and we put the candy on the tree for decoration."

"On the tree? Didn't you eat them?"

"I did, but not until Christmas morning."

"Mommy, could we put some on our tree at home?"

"I think that can be arranged." She grinned.

After they parked, she and Wyatt walked hand in hand toward the town square, stopping to admire the many store displays. Bobby skipped ahead, calling to them excitedly at each new arrangement.

Only a few months ago, she'd come back home to Sierra Creek. With Granny gone, no one had welcomed her. Happiness appeared to be an impossible dream. After living in the city, she wasn't sure she'd fit in the sleepy little village. She shook her head, no point in thinking about the past. The sadness was over. The daydream of having a place of her own had come true. Sierra Creek would always be her home.

"We better hurry. We don't want to miss the tree lighting." Wyatt pulled her toward the town square.

Mayor Breen stood at the bandstand surrounded by the town council. They were all bundled in their best winter coats and each wore a Santa hat. Large multi-colored balls hung from the rafters of the small stage. The area was filled with people waiting for the Christmas tree lights to go on.

The mayor cleared his throat and tapped the microphone he held. "Can everyone hear me?" Feedback screeched. "Millard, please turn the sound down," he said to a hidden worker and tapped the mic again. "As many of you know, I'm Mayor Dan

Breen. I want to congratulate all the merchants and volunteers who worked so hard to make the town more spectacular this year than last year."

Polite applause.

"What's so special about this year?" someone shouted.

"I'm glad you asked. The square was refurbished and it looks great. And once again, Granny's Organic Farm has provided us with a tree."

"I see Amy McCarthy Long in the audience. She's taken over the responsibility of running her grandmother's farm since Granny, Mary McCarthy, passed. Amy supplied this spectacular Christmas tree. Come on up and take a bow, Amy."

She shook her head, no.

"Looks like she didn't hear us. Amy, come on up. Ladies and gentlemen, give her a round of applause."

"Go." Wyatt gave her a nudge.

Reluctantly, she did what she was told.

"Amy, I met your grandmother years ago. As you know, she's donated a tree to Sierra Creek for nigh on to thirty years. Never missed a year. This time, I thought the town might have to buy one. But you stepped up, keeping her legacy. The town folks want to show their appreciation to you and Granny."

"Thank you." She started to leave.

"Hold on, Amy. I'm not finished with you yet."

"You're not?"

"Nope."

The audience laughed.

"We're here to honor your grandmother," Dan Breen continued.

"Thank you."

"Amy, for decades, Granny not only gave us the Christmas tree for the square but without fanfare, donated her time and money to help feed and clothe Sierra Creek citizens who needed a little help, no questions asked." He took a quick breath. "Many of the people here tonight benefited from her big-heartedness. She set an example of kindness we should all try to follow."

There was a spattering of applause.

"Now, I'm proud to name this square, The Mary McCarthy Town Park." He unveiled a brass plaque with her granny's name engraved on it.

The crowd applauded loudly.

Amy's cheeks burned, but her heart filled with pride for her precious Granny. "My grandmother would be surprised and extremely flattered that you gave her this honor."

Wild applauses.

"I understand everyone is waiting for the tree lighting," the mayor shouted. "Amy please do the honors.' He pointed to a switch. "Pull this lever."

When she did, cheers came from the people as lights sparkled on the twenty-foot tree and the high school band started to play, and carolers sang.

As Amy left the park, the townspeople thanked her and wished her a Merry Christmas.

\*\*\*

Later that night on the farm, Wyatt lit a fire in the fireplace and plugged in the Christmas decorations in the living room. "Bobby had a great time."

Amy set two mugs of decaf on the table. "He sure did. I've never seen him so excited. It was hard settling him down for bed—do you want pie?"

"I'm fine." He stood away from the flames and reached for a mug and took a couple of gulps and set it back on the table. He tossed a throw from the couch on the floor, took a couple of decorator pillows and set them on top of the blanket. "Join me. Nice and warm in front of the fire."

She straightened her white sweater, sat next to him, and leaned her head on his shoulder. His strong arm embraced her. The winter chill disappeared, replaced by heat stirring deep within her.

"Wyatt, you knew about naming the square for Granny. It was your idea."

"Mine and many of the town's people. Granny happened to be well-liked. She helped me when I was a kid. Guess she did a lot of good for other people too because the whole town council rallied around using her name."

"I didn't realize."

She sat in silence, sipping coffee and enjoying his company.

"The house is beautiful. You and Bobby did a great job with the decorations."

"Thanks, I want this holiday to be special— Wyatt, I understand you have to go back on the circuit for a few days. This time you'll be back for Christmas Eve dinner. Won't you?"

"Amy, honey, wild horses couldn't keep me away."

***

Amy stretched in bed. *Christmas Eve. Wyatt will be home in time for dinner tonight.*

"Merry Christmas, Mommy," Bobby yelled, running into the bedroom and jumping on the bed.

"Take it easy, big guy. The doctor said to be careful until your scar is healed."

"But I feel happy. Daddy will be here tonight."

"Yeah. I'm happy too." Amy gave him a gentle hug. And this time wild horses wouldn't keep Wyatt away.

As planned, she dropped Bobby off at Sophie's and went to complete the last-minute shopping.

Sophie and Vanna will bring him home when they come to the farm to help with Christmas Eve dinner.

Christmas day, she looked forward to spending time with Wyatt and Bobby. They'd eat leftovers and celebrate the day together, just the three of them—a family.

In Sierra Creek, she found a parking space in front of the Hitching Post and parked the old Volvo. Mr. Smith, the owner of the tack and feed store, opened the place so she could pick up the hand-tooled silver saddle medallions he made, with Wyatt's initials on them. Wyatt had admired Smith's craftmanship, but she knew he would never purchase anything so extravagant for himself; yet he could be so generous to others.

Afterward, she joined the line of people waiting at the local meat market for their organic turkeys.

Down the street, the bakery didn't usually carry gluten-free cookies. Even so, Klaus Mueller, the baker, made them for Bobby. Several cookies were decorated with a red Santa's and the others had green trees. "Bobby will be thrilled. 'Merry Christmas, Klaus."

She carried the packages to the car. If nothing unforeseen happened, dinner would be ready on time.

Granny's silver-plated utensils were already shined and her grandmother's precious bone china of cream with tiny pink roses and a thin gold band waited to be used.

Amy showered, slipped into her underwear, dried her hair, applied mascara, and lipstick. With no budget to buy anything new, she pulled on the green velvet, knee-length dress she'd worn for Christmas the last two years. However, it was still in good condition.

Her last bit of business was to close the clasp on her grandmother's crystal heart necklace. Then she stepped into her black flats.

The sound of music and laughter wafted from downstairs. Bobby must have used his key to let Sophie and Vanna into the house.

She ran downstairs and shouted, "Merry Christmas," and then hugged each one.

"I brought what you asked for and Johnny sent fresh vegetables from his winter garden. The carrots are beautiful," Sophie said.

"Wonderful."

In the kitchen, Amy stopped to take a selfie of the three women all wearing Christmas aprons of red cotton with silver bells on them. The ones Sophie had sewn.

"We have to snap a photo while the aprons are clean." Amy laughed. "They're beautiful. It would be a shame to get anything on them."

"Don't be silly. That's what they're made for," Sophie responded, always the practical one.

"Well, they're beautiful and you are too." She hugged the woman.

"Better get to work if we want dinner on the table," Sophie reprimanded her, but Amy saw a glimmer of a smile in her eyes.

"Well, if we're going to work, we need more music. Something we can dance to." Vanna tuned in the "Top 40" from her cell phone app and swayed to the beat.

Bobby jumped from his chair at the table and began to dance with Vanna. She twirled him to the kitchen sink and filled a large bowl with water. "You're such a big guy, Bobby. I bet you can wash the potatoes and put them in the pot."

He grinned and went to work. Amy chopped apples from the farm and soon the kitchen filled with the aroma of apple pies cooking in the oven.

Sophie put on a tape of Granny's favorite Christmas songs sung by popular artists of her generation and everyone sang along.

For a moment, it was as if her grandmother was there in the kitchen working beside them. Granny was humming and then singing the wrong words as she always used to, before laughing at her mistakes. Only to begin singing again, as soon as the next song started. Recalling those days, Amy smiled.

The pies, apple and pumpkin, were out and the turkey was in the oven. They prepared the onions, carrots and other vegetables Johnny sent, his contribution to the feast. Wyatt was set to arrive in time for dinner.

"Have you set a date for the wedding?" Vanna asked.

"Not yet. Wyatt's been on the circuit, so we haven't had a chance to talk about it. Sometimes I can't believe it's happening." Amy glanced out of the kitchen window at the darkened sky. A second later, thunder cracked, shaking the house.

It was followed by a huge downpour. The wind seemed to appear from nowhere and hail bounced off the roof. Not the white Christmas Amy had hoped for, but still, it was white.

Bobby ran to the window and peered out. "Wow, hail. Mommy, can we make a snowman with hail?"

"I'm not sure, honey."

"We better get the dining table set," Sophie shouted over the sound of the wind.

"You run a tight ship." Amy grinned.

"I can attest to that," Vanna agreed.

"Well, that's how to get the job done," Sophie said, defending herself.

"Point made," Amy said. "Don't take it the wrong way. We're only teasing you."

Sophie smiled. "Come on, Bobby. I can use your help in the dining room."

\*\*\*

Hours later, the turkey was ready, as were the mashed potatoes and vegetables. Amy stared out the kitchen window into the freezing rain and wished for the roar of the Ford pickup truck coming up the driveway.

The clock on the kitchen wall caught her attention. If she didn't serve the meal soon, it would be spoiled. The dinner would start without Wyatt.

Disbelief shook her. She'd have bet the world he'd be here tonight. But he was doing it again, no call, no text, nothing. He had bailed on her again, leaving her to face their friends and Bobby alone. How could she explain him being a "no show?"

She wouldn't cry. Not this time. The diamond on her engagement ring sparkled on her finger and she resisted the urge to take it off. How had she let Wyatt hurt her once more? Stupid was too kind a word for what she was.

The sound of laughter and Christmas Carols came from the living room. Before returning to her guests, she forced a smile.

"Have you heard from Wyatt?" Vanna whispered.

"No."

Later, everyone sat in the dining room. All said the table looked beautiful. She lit the candles and Johnny agreed to carve the turkey. But tension filled the room as their eyes avoided Wyatt's empty chair.

*Not the perfect holiday dinner I dreamed of. Still, I won't let Wyatt spoil it.*

Bobby said grace and they were about to eat when the doorbell rang.

"Excuse me. I'll be right back." She quickly left the room. *Who can be at the door on Christmas Eve?*

"I'm coming," she shouted.

Amy opened the front door and saw a cowboy Santa standing at the front door carrying a large bag over his shoulder.

Wet head to toe, the red Santa hat he wore dripping with rain, Wyatt grinned. "The back door was locked. I couldn't get in. Sorry I'm late. Couldn't call, the damn cell phone battery went dead. I hit a patch of black ice on the highway and had to leave the truck in a ditch and walk home."

"Oh God, are you hurt?"

"No, just late."

"I thought you didn't care and weren't coming."

He stared, a shocked expression on his handsome face. "Amy, I thought you understood, I love you." He dropped his bag and reached to wipe her tears. "I told you wild horses couldn't keep me from being here tonight."

She threw her arms around him.

"Amy, I'm soaking wet!"

"I don't care. I love you too."

"Merry Christmas, honey." He hugged her.

"Merry Christmas, Wyatt, my country heart."

***** 

Hope you enjoyed this book, please help the author and other readers by leaving a positive review on Amazon, Bookbub.com, etc. BTW, 5-star reviews are greatly appreciated. Thank you.

To find out what happens to Amy and Wyatt read **His Country Heart Sierra Creek Book 2**

Read Vanna's story in **Our Country Heart Sierra Creek Book 3.**

**My Country Heart book 4, meet the new people in town as they become acquainted with Amy, Wyatt, and the people in Sierra Creek.**

**If suspense is your thing, check out Dangerous Web part of the Dangerous Series by Reggi Allder.**

## ABOUT THE AUTHOR

**Reggi Allder** writes contemporary small-town romance and suspense. They are all stand-alone books. She studied creative writing and screenwriting at the University of California Los Angeles (UCLA).

She enjoys hearing from her readers.
**Reggiallder.com Follow her on** Bookbub.com and
like her on Facebook

# Books by Reggi Allder

**Sierra Creek Series:**
Her Country Heart
His Country Heart
Our Country Heart
My Country Heart

**Dangerous Series:**
Dangerous Web
Dangerous Denial
Dangerous Money
Dangerous Moves
**Coming next:** Dangerous Sisters

**Other books:**
Shattered Rules
With Glowing Hearts

www.ingramcontent.com/pod-product-compliance
Lightning Source LLC
Chambersburg PA
CBHW060906250626

47159CB00008B/2886